PENGUIN SCIENCE FICTION

ARROWS OF DESIR

Born in 1900, Geoffrey House _____ _____ ___ated at Clifton and Magdalen College, Oxford, and, after taking a First in English, spent four years as a banker in Romania. Irked by the tedium of it he set off for Spain to market bananas, and from there went on to the United States just in time for the Depression. After writing children's plays for radio in the States he returned to England, but shortly afterwards began to travel printers' inks in Europe and South America. Meanwhile *Atlantic Monthly* encouraged him to start writing professionally, on the strength of his short stories. His first novel, *The Third Hour*, was published in 1937 and was followed by a collection of short stories. He was unable to profit by the success of *Rogue Male* (to which *Rogue Justice* is the sequel), published in 1939, since he had already been despatched to Romania as an Intelligence Officer by the time it came out. He remained in the Middle East until 1945 and then almost had to begin again as a writer. Since then he has published many novels as well as short stories, among them are *A Rough Shoot*, *A Time to Kill*, *Watcher in the Shadows*, *Thing to Love*, *Olura*, *The Courtesy of Death*, *Dance of the Dwarfs*, *The Three Sentinels*, *The Lives and Times of Bernardo Brown*, *Red Anger*, *Hostage: London*, *The Sending* and *Summon the Bright Water*. He has also written several books for children, including *The Exploits of Xenophon*, *Prisoner of the Indies* and *Escape into Daylight*. His autobiography is entitled *Against the Wind*.

Geoffrey Household is married and lives in Buckinghamshire.

ARROWS
OF DESIRE

Geoffrey Household

PENGUIN BOOKS

Penguin Books Ltd, Harmondsworth, Middlesex, England
Viking Penguin Inc., 40 West 23rd Street, New York, New York 10010, U.S.A.
Penguin Books Australia Ltd, Ringwood, Victoria, Australia
Penguin Books Canada Ltd, 2801 John Street, Markham, Ontario, Canada L3R 1B4
Penguin Books (N.Z.) Ltd, 182–190 Wairau Road, Auckland 10, New Zealand

First published by Michael Joseph Ltd 1985
Published in Penguin Books 1987

Printed and bound in Great Britain by
Cox & Wyman Ltd, Reading

Chapter I

Pezulu Pasha, the Chief of Police, was fiddling with his uniform hat, a tall shako made of white fur and lined with red silk, folding it with an air of regret and once jabbing a blunt forefinger through two holes just below the crown. An imperious hat it was, which should have been worn upright as a lighthouse, flashing in front the springing silver sapling which was the emblem of the Euro-African Federation. Tito Pezulu, however, always cocked it jauntily at an angle as if to emphasise that he

1

was no stiff bureaucrat but a dashing leader of governed and governors alike.

'I was fond of that hat,' he complained. 'It's made of real fur from a forest animal. Humphrey of Middlesex gave it to me.'

'The bullet was meant for me, not you,' the High Commissioner said abstractedly.

The futility of the act depressed him. Assassination was so useless. The State had only to buy itself a replacement and carry on. The proprietor of a puppet show was not going to give up business because a puppet was smashed.

'Perhaps, sir. After all, there would be little point in removing me and landing themselves with a new man who didn't know the country.'

Tito Pezulu was convinced that the immigrants liked him. His attitude had always been paternal and his complexion was not very different from that of a sunburnt, weatherbeaten Briton, contrasting with the clear-cut distinguished features of the much darker High Commissioner. But in fact the immigrants didn't like him. Ali Pretorius was sure of that. Pezulu was patronising rather than paternal.

The High Commissioner got up from his great ebony desk, passed through the crimson rope which so unnecessarily separated him from callers, and stared out of the east window – an occasional compulsion to which normally he only surrendered when he was alone – unsure whether he was trying to concentrate thought or to avoid it.

The windows of his office in the Residency looked down over the public gardens and white streets of

Avebury and up again to the factories and satellite communities on the Marlborough Downs. Old were the sites and would have remained nameless if not for the canvas-backed maps treasured by British antiquarians which, unlike paper, were still legible. Tradition insisted that there had been some great sanctuary on that high, clear ground so obviously suited to habitation, yet no sign of it was left beyond inexplicable tall stones and curious hillocks bearing little resemblance to the ragged mounds within the forest which were indeed the impenetrable remains of cities.

Avebury and its suburbs could not, he assured himself, be so very different from other new towns of the Euro-African Federation. They stood so sanely, only requiring benevolent administration, above the southern forests which rolled away in great billows of oak and ash netted by the lianas of ivy and bramble, pierced by no roads and revealing no silver flash of water from the many little rivers. All problems down there were for the future, for the ecologists, planners and engineers, as soon as this policy of resettlement was plainly succeeding.

What had done the most damage to this remnant of a once great people? Was it the exile or the return? At the end of the Age of Destruction there had not been much more than half a million left alive: a mere handful to refuse uniform development when all the former nations of Europe and the shores of the Mediterranean had huddled together in horror, determined to renounce in perpetuity their former nationalities and political systems. But the British had refused and Armed Persuasion had to be used; it was discontinued when the supposed population had been reduced by half.

The disease of primitive nationalism proved, however, ineradicable, and in the year 2241 reappeared in its most deadly form of guerrilla warfare against the Federation. When at last the insurgents surrendered, the remaining British were resettled in North Africa, while the island, like the scheduled deserts scattered throughout Asia and the Americas, was proclaimed radioactive and uninhabitable. The small parties of natives who had slunk away into the spreading forests with their last pathetic dregs of animals were abandoned to decline and extinction.

Exile, Pretorius believed, had been the mistake which had inspired them to preserve in private their customs and codes and fanciful traditions. Instead of accepting the happy placidity of normal welfare units, they had remained a people apart, arousing such prejudices that the Supreme Council, in one of those spasms of sentiment so liable to affect popular assemblies, permitted the resettlement of the island to celebrate the year 3000. The first colony and the seat of government were established at Avebury, a newly built city surrounded by agreeable industrial estates. As their High Commissioner it was his duty to suppress any revival of nationalism while at the same time tolerating their myths and peculiarities. His administration ought to resemble a nursery school rather than a police court.

That was a vision never to be expressed with such crudity outside his own mind; but the wings of truth were in it, even if singed by a passing bullet. Ali Pretorius, staring from his window at the lines of white houses and public buildings climbing the opposite slopes like a procession of happy children,

4

confirmed the would-be ideal of his administration.

He turned back from the window to the muscular mass of Pezulu Pasha confidently jammed in the chair opposite the Caesarian desk. He envied the strength and single-mindedness of his Chief of Police – or any Chief of Police if it came to that. To enforce the law was so much more easy than to question it.

'I want to talk to this girl myself,' he said.

Pezulu objected that no examining psychologist had yet seen her.

'There's plenty of time for that. I want her as she is, not as she will be.'

'Very risky, sir. The sooner you let me nip her over to North Africa, the better. You know what their underground press is like. If you do an interrogation yourself, they'll say you beat her up.'

'My dear Tito, they have known me for two years as their High Commissioner. If after that they can say or even think that I would beat anybody up, then nothing matters any more.'

'Well, if you insist. But I would like a neutral witness to be present.'

'Sometimes I feel that in all this island I am the only neutral.'

'You mustn't take it to heart, sir. What I mean by a neutral witness is one of their people, but in our pay.'

The attempt on the High Commissioner had taken place when he stepped out into a patch of sunshine after inaugurating the new Museum of Science. The polygonal terrace in front of the new building was surrounded by a balustrade with a lion rampant at each of the corners. Lions and pilasters were decorated by wreaths and wands of flowers in the green and red of the Federation.

This display had been organised by the Council of Communal Design, an ineffective but well-meaning body which considered itself above the inelegance of political action. Helpers had been recruited from the College of Arts, noted for an unruliness hitherto only expressed in satirical pamphlets and impudent graffiti. *Pezulu Out* from the members' lavatory at the Trade Institute had been photographed by the Faculty of Communal Design, and its cartoon of Pezulu making water in his hat had been exhibited – in private – as an example of excellence in script and colour. Pezulu had been amused, and now blamed himself for failing to appreciate that among these students might be cells dedicated to action as well as art.

The would-be assassin was a girl in her late teens. Her wand of flowers concealed an old-fashioned rifle which, seen at a distance, was of a shape not immediately familiar to populace and police. Its accuracy made it an ideal weapon since it did not have to be programmed for any required intimidation, and the single bullet, directed at an individual by sight alone, could kill.

Kneeling in the cover of a richly garlanded lion, she had fired the shot which narrowly missed the High Commissioner and scored on Tito Pezulu's hat. Arrested before she could mix with the crowd, she maintained that she had acted alone. However, no rifle was missing from the Sporting Club and she could never had laid her hands on such an obsolete but accurate weapon without the help of some underground organisation.

* * *

Those lines of uniformly cheerful houses which had so comforted Pretorius by their air of peace and placidity rarely showed much evidence of individual taste; but one of them, at the end of its terrace, had an undefinable air of solidity which might have been due to the squareness of the front lawn or the hinged front door instead of the usual sliding panel, or simply to the fact that the federal tenant, Alfred Brown, was a respectable and prominent member of the Town Assembly.

The living room looked east over the rolling grassland which in the distance met the threatening forest as a beach meets the sea. It was clean and functional as a hospital cell, with all furniture and domestic machinery concealed behind the wall panels. Even the table and the seating could be made to disappear if not required. Yet Alfred Brown, as if to remind himself of that other Britain, had cluttered up the place with fake mementos from the antique dealers of North Africa. There was a grandfather clock with no face, a mahogany commode, its true use forgotten, with a tasselled cover of rotting embroidery and a clumsy, ornate dresser of plastic wood, its scrolls and garlands moulded rather than carved. It pleased Alfred to show in this harmless manner a respect for the past which could hardly be proscribed as nationalism. Mrs Brown complained that she couldn't clean the place because one of his treasures was always in the way. She preferred their life in North Africa and said so, but love and loyalty had forced her to give way to husband and daughter.

In that living room, a week before the unparalleled assault on Tito Pezulu's hat, Silvia Brown was sitting at her father's table with two male companions both at

7

least ten years older than herself. She had been told from babyhood that she was a perfect example of the old British type. Neighbours on the African housing estate where she was brought up used to call on her parents just to look at her. Deep blue eyes and golden hair were very uncommon owing to centuries of intermarriage.

In spite of all this adulation Silvia Brown was in no way conceited. She had given herself to the cause of her people with comparatively humble dedication; the nearest she ever came to romanticising herself was sometimes, when waking in a desolate first light, to enter on a half-dreamed communion with Britannia – that mythical figure who turned up in fragments of Old English poetry and was believed by some to have been a Goddess of the Ocean, by others a forgotten heroine of the Age of Destruction. After her parents had come out to the island with the second wave of immigrants, Silvia had been much in demand for festivals and pageants until the police closed them down as contributing to nationalism. She was undoubtedly a joy to British eyes, though too tall and muscular for the more delicate taste of the Federation.

Her two companions did not look markedly British; in the street they could well have been taken for government employees. Unit Green was thin and a little bent, perhaps a schoolmaster, perhaps an associate of the Society of Mathematicians trying to deduce from charred fragments of equations theories of the Universe only intelligible to physicists who had been dead a thousand years.

Green was indeed an expert in extending knowledge,

but of a more mundane nature. He was a master printer who produced and distributed the *Avebury Clarion*, a harmless weekly organ which chronicled the social news, the rare crimes and entertainments of the immigrant community together with the births and deaths and licences to produce children. The paper was patronised by the High Commissioner himself, who would occasionally contribute a witty light essay. Its full contents, however, were only known to selected subscribers and newsagents, and could be obtained by ironing flat the wrapping paper in which parcels of the *Clarion* were delivered. A news sheet specially printed for British eyes then appeared; it had nothing to do with births and licences but by no means excluded desirable deaths.

At the table discussion had come to a halt. The third person broke the momentary silence.

'Then the only question left is: which of us?'

A common enough type of organiser was Unit Smith, thin-lipped, the eyes expressionless and lacking any obvious right to fire and dominate his companions.

'I am sorry to open it all up again, Smith, but I still do not agree with the timing,' Green objected. 'The proposed action has not been well enough integrated with my propaganda campaign.'

The white calm which hid the tension and ability of Smith changed to a calm white heat.

'You've no choice, mate. The committee approved the timing and we are delegated to take action.'

'I'm tired of them.'

'Of course! So am I. But you intellectuals never understand that the object of a committee is to take responsibility for whatever has been decided before it meets.'

Silvia Brown asked impatiently if they hadn't talked long enough. Smith silently agreed with her, for he could answer his own question and already knew very well who would fire the shot. He could congratulate himself on the imperceptible manoeuvres by which he had ensured that Silvia Brown would be available and willing. How invaluable was that saintly delirium of youth dedicated to an ideal! Silvia and her cell of students were blindly scornful of all conventional scruples and could be sacrificed with no great loss to the movement. Green, that precious fellow who seemed to believe that words were action, must not be allowed to take the edge off the girl.

'Dear friend,' he said, 'none of us will ever forget the wonderful clarity with which you seconded the motion. You told us that if we killed a High Commissioner who was a stupid, cruel brute, all the liberals in the Federation would start yapping that he deserved it. And so our protest would be lost. But when we wipe out a generous, futile official like Pretorius it will be plain that our protest is not against him but against our treatment by the Federation.'

'And I don't take back a word of it! But you confused me when you suddenly asked who would do it.'

'Who did you think would do it?' Silvia exclaimed. 'Your office boy?'

Unit Green half rose from his chair but then decided that humility would be a more fitting retort than rebuke.

'It was only the timing which I doubted, Silvia. But

when that is agreed I am quite prepared to do the job myself. If caught I shall not be missed.'

Smith brought him down to earth.

'No "if" about it! A prominent citizen, and on the terrace armed!'

But in the confusion Silvia might not be noticed before she could escape; that he had foreseen before selecting her. He waited for her to volunteer.

'I shall be in the party which decorates the terrace,' she said. 'I could hide the weapon in an armful of tall flowers.'

Smith pretended horror. It could not be allowed. She was too young.

'But it must be me. You are too valuable to be risked. And dear old Green here – I'll bet he can't shoot straight.'

'I'll jump out and stick a knife in him.'

'Before Pezulu gets you?' Silvia asked. 'And you wouldn't look right kneeling behind a sheaf of chrysan-themums. I would.'

Silly old things rifles were, but shooting with them was still taught in the Sporting Club like fencing and archery; and when she shot at a target she imagined that she was a freedom fighter at some battle in the past. At the Club, however, rifles and even bows were kept locked up to discourage similar fantasies. She had not a hope of smuggling one through the security checks.

'Can you provide the weapon?' she asked Smith.

'Three of them to choose from if you can hide them here.'

The High Commissioner, determined to carry out a

dispassionate interrogation of Silvia Brown himself, glanced through the tray of cards from official callers expressing their regrets and apologies in the hope of finding the neutral witness required by Pezulu. Summoning his ADC, he asked if any of them were still out in the anteroom.

He had deliberately picked young Julian Cola to accompany him to Avebury, well aware that he was going to need some cheerful associate who took nothing too seriously. Julian filled the bill. He was devoted, dependable and outwardly irresponsible.

'Sorry the hat has sprung a leak, Chief!' Julian said, with a courtly nod to Pezulu. 'Well, sir, the Assembly has gone into special session so the Mayor and the Chairman of Committees have had to leave to take their seats. They hate to lose their attendance money. The Chancellor of the Exchequer is still hanging around.'

'He'll do.'

'No, sir. Not that crafty old hypocrite!' Pezulu protested.

'The immigrants respect him, Tito. What he says goes. He's the sort of leader the plain man admires.'

'As if anyone knew what an exchequer was or why it had a chancellor!'

'All their titles are meaningless. But the British like to preserve the prestige of vanished power.'

Yes, but prestige could recreate power. Pretorius was perplexed by so alien a figure. The Chancellor was corrupt in everything but money, yet he was treated as if he were a sort of priest, a survival from the days before all organised religion had faded away. History, he remembered, showed that politicians when promising the impossible had frequently declared themselves inspired by a divine purpose.

'Show him in, Julian, will you? And then I want this Silvia Brown here.'

The Chancellor made his entry with outstretched arm and hand, nicely calculated to show eagerness without loss of dignity. Theatre – all theatre! But so was this stern and noble residence on its bare hill; so was the automatic, ceremonious opening of that massive double door of British oak set in its immense and superfluous frame of rare woods from Africa. Pretorius preferred simplicity. It occurred to him that nowhere in Avebury, not even in this Silvia Brown, was he likely to find it.

Undeniably the so-called Chancellor was an imposing figure. He wore a light brown beard, a fashion rare among Euro-Africans though common enough among visitors from the Federations of Asia and the Americas. Above it his wide eyes were blue as ocean and as restless. Tunic and trousers were deep purple instead of the pale colours worn by the ordinary citizens, and he was draped in an open black frock coat from shoulder to knees.

The Chancellor acknowledged the presence of the Chief of Police by no more than a formal inclination of the head.

'Your Excellency! My dear colleague! I am appalled. I cannot express my horror.'

Pretorius rose to meet him, shook the clammy hand and remarked that it was very kind of him to call.

'And I have come not only to assure you of my own sorrow but of that of all my lambs at this attempt against

Your Excellency, and to offer you our heartfelt congratulations on your happy escape.'

'So it *was* him she aimed at, not me,' Pezulu pointed out with satisfaction.

'I ... I assumed ... my assumption was perhaps ... No, no, I cannot affirm their intentions. The commission of this act of violence –' the Chancellor recovered his composure '– this vicious deed upon the holiday which sanctifies the month of August, this is what shames me. On that holiday no manner of work shall be done. The very foundation of the British creed!'

'You would describe assassination as work?' Pretorius asked, partly to restore a conversational tone and partly because he was genuinely interested.

'No activity but ball play is permitted.'

'Like that cricket of yours. A most interesting dance. My daughter – she's studying British folklore for her doctorate, you know – believes that the twenty-two men are celebrating the successful decontamination of a strip of cultivated ground.'

'We do not know the origin. It is a custom written in the Laws of Nelson and hallowed by the centuries.'

Pezulu remarked that they might obey a few other laws while they were at it.

'A passing phase. Merely a passing phase,' the Chancellor replied. 'When at last my lambs have self-government ...'

'Do you have to call them your lambs?'

'From the old expression, pasha, to fleece the lambs. That, from time immemorial, has been the duty of the Chancellor of the Exchequer: to love them, to care for their welfare, in fact to fleece them for their good.'

14

The High Commissioner resumed his official chair and motioned to the two to sit opposite.

'Chancellor, I am anxious to talk to this Silvia Brown myself. Would you mind very much if I asked you to be present?'

'I hope and pray that your Excellency does not consider ...'

'Of course not! Innocence, collusion – in politics the words have no precise meaning. What matters is that I'm dealing with bitterness and want to understand it. Tito, ask your Inspector to bring her in!'

The Inspector escorted Silvia Brown from the guard room, remaining by the door with a professionally blank face and abandoning his prisoner to stand alone in this spacious room empty of all but the insignia of power. Pretorius was astonished by her air of defiance, by that gentle face which seemed carved in marble, by her youth. He had never thought much of his own skill as an interrogator. Should he try the stern approach of an offended parent? Oh, nonsense! Then treat the girl as any other, with normal courtesy.

He rose, unhooked a section of that absurd rope which divided him from humanity and asked the Inspector to bring in a chair.

'Do come closer and sit down, Miss Brown.'

'I will not.'

'Well, you have a perfect right to refuse to speak to me. And if you wish to leave this room at once, you are free to do so.'

'I am not afraid of you.'

As she obviously was, Pretorius smiled at her and sat informally on the corner of his desk.

'There's no reason at all why you should be,' he said.

Silvia ignored him and asked the Chancellor if he was under arrest too.

Pezulu answered for him: 'Not yet.'

'I asked the Chancellor to be present so that you would not feel alone among enemies,' Pretorius said, pointedly ignoring his Chief of Police.

'I am never alone. The Britons and all their past are in the room with me.'

'I, too, sometimes have that feeling, Miss Brown. One cannot govern without affection creeping in.'

A perfectly sincere remark without ulterior motive, but it did the trick. She moved closer to him out of the emptiness of the great room, but did not sit down.

'What do you want to know?' she asked.

'Whether I have incurred your personal dislike.'

'I am the servant of my people. I have no likes or dislikes.'

'I see. You were – well – shooting at the Federation, shall we say? But suppose you had hit some innocent bystander? Think of the remorse if your bullet had gone through Pezulu Pasha's head instead of his hat!'

Silvia could not help smiling.

'He'd do fine to go on with,' she said.

The Chancellor moaned piously that such an answer was most indecorous.

'Federation out! Britain for ever!'

'My dear young lady, keep your slogans for the street!' Pretorius ordered. 'The Federation has decided that the British Welfare units shall become free partners in not less than fifty and not more than one hundred

16

years. Violent revolt will not make the slightest difference.'

'It will!'

'Against the united power of Euro-Africa? How?'

'Because there are thousands of us to take my place. I am only one, and what you do to me does not matter.'

'Miss Brown, I cannot sympathise with pretentious nonsense. What the penal psychiatrists will do to you is probably no more than mate and children would do in any case.'

'No! I demand my right to die by the rope.'

'Rope?'

'It was the custom of our ancestors,' the Chancellor explained.

'He's quite right,' said Pezulu. 'I read it in their history somewhere. They took a rope like this, you see,' – he picked up from the floor the end of the ornamental rope – 'and made a loop round the neck and another round the ankles and pulled at both ends until something gave. It must have solved a lot of problems.'

'I cannot believe it was done to mere children like her,' the High Commissioner exclaimed in horror.

Silvia Brown faced the man of peace with blazing contempt.

'At the end, seven hundred years ago, it was the children who fought in the last streets!'

'I cannot understand why. There has never been so impossible a people in all history.'

'There has!'

'Your evidence?'

'A fragment in the religious anthology.'

17

'And which, dear lamb, is that?' the Chancellor asked.

Silvia Brown answered slowly and with tears in her eyes:

'By the waters of Babylon we sat down and wept when we remembered thee, O Sion.'

Pezulu looked at Pretorius for his orders. The High Commissioner shrugged his shoulders helplessly and nodded.

'Back to her cell for care and protection, Inspector,' Pezulu directed.

'Tyrants! Exploiters! Death to Ali Pretorius!'

She threw herself on the floor and went limp. Pezulu made a movement to pull down her skirt which was round her waist, but thought better of it. He beckoned to his Inspector, who dragged her out by the shoulders as gently as possible but with obvious disgust.

'This is most painful. Most painful,' the Chancellor lamented. 'Your Excellency has been very patient.'

'That is what I'm here for. Could you impress it on your people that they too must be patient?'

'Alas, my influence is so limited. And now, if you need me no more ...' He bowed himself out with hands folded on his chest in a gesture of humility.

'The place wants disinfecting,' Pezulu said.

'A good wash would do. He's all right on his own subject. Theodosia thinks he was a sort of high priest in the old days.'

'I believe he invents half their traditions to suit himself.'

'But he hasn't invented this damned ideal of patriotism. They have never lost it and are quite capable of spreading it. It's incredible that a civilised human being can feel any longer as that poor girl did. The children fought in the last streets – my God, does anyone want the nation state ever again?'

'We might oblige her by reviving that death penalty.'

'It was useless in the Russian revolt. There was a streak in their character which made them enjoy it. And I must remind you, Tito,' he added in a less conversational tone, 'that I carry out policy. I do not make it.'

'You do – when there is any.'

That was true. The leisurely Federation never interfered, so that he was left unwillingly with the power of a Caesar. He had not sought the job; nobody would in a world which, apart from small and isolated pockets of discontent, had never felt, had even forgotten the mad craving for war. He remembered how casually, ten minutes late, he had obeyed the summons to the President's office. He had supposed that his advice was wanted on some administrative problem of the North African British; as prefect of their province he was officially presumed to understand their customs. He knew, himself, that he observed rather than understood.

The President had been at his most courteous. One had always to guess from his lengthy, friendly enquiries what his real object was. He referred to a recent pronouncement of the physicists that their science was believed to be now equal to that of the middle twentieth century; he asked after Madam Pretorius' chronic bronchitis; he begged Ali to congratulate his daughter, Theodosia, on the reviews of her monograph on the underground communities of central Russia. Fatherly pride was somewhat diluted by Ali's conviction that Thea had tailored the facts to her interpretation of them.

Then the point of the interview had been gradually approached.

'Ali, what is your considered opinion on the establishment of High Commissions?'

'A successful innovation, sir. But it has never been tested in an emergency.'

'What about the new immigrants in Britain? Would a High Commissioner be right for them?'

'Is one likely to be needed? From all I hear, the elected assembly is a fairly responsible body so far.'

'But better too early than too late.'

'Provided you can lay your hands on the right man.'

'I think I can, my dear Ali. You.'

It was the highest honour. There were only four such High Commissioners in the whole Federation, and those in provinces where the people did not wholly accept the common civilisation and armed Moral Persuasion might have to be used.

The appointment was so unexpected that his mind instantly took refuge in trivialities. His wife ought certainly not to live permanently in those damp Atlantic mists and should limit her visits to short periods; Thea could act as hostess and turn to the obscure forest tribes for her research; he would have to endure a palatial official residence instead of his flowered Moorish villa; police and security thugs would have to be commanded and conciliated though he detested the whole lot of them.

In spite of all this personal reluctance, he heard his

voice accepting with the sense of duty proper to a high government servant:

'It's a great responsibility, sir. I hope I can handle it.'

'Of course you can, my dear Ali. We shall depend on your advice and give you full support. The man on the spot knows best.'

'Yes – provided he also knows his own mind.'

'In case of trouble, you will find Tito Pezulu a great help. We sent him out with the first wave of immigrants and he has been in Avebury ever since.'

Ali Pretorius had doubted then how much help Pezulu was likely to be. Chiefs of Police seldom were, in spite of being storehouses of detailed knowledge. So often they could not see the wood for the trees.

He had been right to doubt. Now, two years later, the immediate future of the British experiment was incalculable, reminding him that science still could not claim infallibility in forecasting the island's weather. He had learned that 'in trouble' – by which the president had meant revolt – he could depend only on himself.

To the Federation, nationalism was the unpardonable crime. It led inevitably to war. The occasional severity of Pezulu and his like was justified. But nationalism resembled a genetic abnormality which could not be bred out of generations of absurd flag-wavers. Some policy, some rule of conduct common to both immigrants and the High Commissioner must exist. Perhaps it could be found not in short-lived humanity but in the earth of this mysterious green and empty land into which all – he and they – had been replanted from the hothouse of the Federation.

Chapter II

Theodosia Pretorius walked slowly back through the parks and playgrounds of Avebury, towards the High Commissioner's residence which dominated the colony. Dominated? The word had slipped into her mind. It was unfair, she thought. The site was slightly higher than its surroundings, but in no way overpowering. The Federation had every reason to be proud of its resettlement of the British, of its grouped houses surrounded by open space, its terraces which mapped the groves and pools, its low factories stretching westwards, their white walls complementing the spaced public buildings in the centre of the city. Could one even call it a city through which she walked? It was a country in miniature, a newborn babe ready to be lifted from the bloodied sheets of the past.

One missed, of course, the great overland transport services of the rest of the Federation, but there was as yet no need for them; the impenetrable wall of the forest was everywhere within sight and walking distance of the colony, its edge a playground for children – their supervision should be improved – who would daringly gather flowers in summer, chestnuts in autumn, and run away.

It was all so well planned for the peace and happiness of the British Welfare Units, yet there was discontent which she could not explain. Her official duties were easy and satisfying, and she was well aware from the eyes which turned towards her that her tawny beauty was admired by the immigrants, prejudiced though they were in favour of blue eyes and colourless hair. Her emotions were untouched and she was consciously glad that there were no eligible and persistent males in her immediate entourage to distract her from ethnology; nor did her recent feeling that two parts of her were not neatly meshed together have anything to do with her work. Of that she was sure. She was fascinated by her research into the culture of the native British, surprisingly homogeneous in spite of the fact that their hidden clearings, scattered obscurely over the island, were connected only by narrow green lanes shaved clean for the stride of couriers and the trotting of shaggy little horses which – disappointingly – did not in the least resemble the noble beasts of old British poetry and romance.

She couldn't attribute her vague self-questioning to the British Welfare Units through whose midst she had passed for the last hour and a half, genially if a little critically. Their culture and manners were exactly the same as they had been in North Africa, though they puzzled her kindly father rather more than before. Those antique ideals which he had found merely comic he now studied more closely. Now that the exiles had come home, as they called it, there was a risk of nationalism. Theodosia could not believe that it was serious. There was nothing that the immigrants, happy in permanent peace and the warmth of the Federal beehive, could desire that they had not already got.

She passed through the imposing arch which gave access to the Residency, saluted by a policeman with his mouth full; then through the inner gate where an untidy guard also saluted while adjusting his belt with his spare hand. An absurd and pointless tradition! How could one expect smartness when the wearer of the uniform felt that there would never again be war in which smartness was essential?

Seeing that lobbies and anteroom were empty of petitioners, chairmen of committees and other British time-wasters, she entered her father's hall of audience and found him sitting rather grimly with his detestable Chief of Police.

'Where have you been?' he asked as if, wherever it was, it should have been somewhere else.

'Sitting on a tree trunk and probing Humphrey.'

'Humphrey?'

'Humphrey of Middlesex.'

'Oh, him! Did he give you that licence to enter his tribal reserve?'

'Of course he did. They've just made a landing strip in a forest glade. I shall fly in at the end of the week.'

'He's reliable, you think?' Pretorius asked Tito Pezulu.

'Charming fellow!' Pezulu answered heartily. 'He dislikes the immigrants as much as we do.'

'Why are they behaving so oddly on the August holiday?' Theodosia asked. 'So many of them seemed to be moving on the centre.'

'A special meeting of their Assembly. Somebody, I'm afraid ... er ... shot at me.'

'And hit my hat, by God!' Pezulu exclaimed.

Theodosia threw her arms round her father and kissed him, crying that they must be quite mad. Pezulu, smiling benevolently on the touching scene as if he had been the rescuer, showed her the holes in his hat.

'They'll have to give you another decoration for that,' Theodosia said.

Pretorius, knowing his daughter, remarked quickly and tactfully that it was long overdue.

'I wouldn't like it, sir, just for being at the wrong end of a firearm!'

'But, my dear Tito,' Theodosia purred sweetly, 'it's impossible for *you* to receive anything you don't deserve.'

The double-edged compliment was quite lost on

25

Pezulu, as she was sure it would be, and he continued complacently:

'Well, it did show my organisation was sound. I had two men just behind her ...'

'A woman? How could she? What was she like?'

'Fine looking creature in her way. Good legs, too! My agents whipped her out of the crowd the moment she had fired ...'

'Couldn't they have done it the moment before?'

'That's too much to expect of security men, Miss Thea. They must have eyes everywhere, you see.'

'What will be done with her, my father?'

'Just deported to Africa for correction. The fanatics are very few and we must avoid turning them into martyrs.'

'The masses are all with us, but they daren't say so,' Pezulu added.

'And they know that the economic position of a self-governing Britain would be impossible.'

Parrot talk? Theodosia was about to say that no excitable populace had ever given two hoots for its economic position, when Julian Cola entered and confirmed it for her.

'The result of the special session of the Town Assembly is through, sir.'

'Thank you, Julian. We'll send them the usual kind message this evening.'

'I'm afraid the left wing carried an amendment against the Executive.'

'That's what left wings are for, dear Julian. What was the final motion?'

'That this House repudiates the use of violence in the

pursuit of self-government, while solemnly warning the Federation that its policy must inevitably result in violence.'

'So now at last we know!' Pezulu said, putting on his hat at its most dashing angle. 'State of Readiness, sir?'

'No! Not yet!' The High Commissioner hesitated and then more firmly repeated: 'Not yet! Julian, you will accompany the Chief of Police as my personal representative and report directly to me.'

When they had left, Theodosia tried to reassure her father. She knew only too well how he resented his own images of himself: both the strong man and the too tolerant.

'If *you* couldn't prevent it, nobody could.'

'Whatever those damned policemen say, I won't believe that if we treat the immigrants graciously they will not be gracious. Perhaps that is a sort of tyranny – to force affection on them.'

'Because they are already in love.'

'What on earth do you mean, Thea?'

'It's hard to put into words. They love Britain just as if it were a person.'

'But Units can't love a country. They can feel a cordial respect for a government or system, but not for a slab of geography.'

'What do you feel about our villa in Agadir?'

'I love it.'

'Well, there you are!'

'But that's a very small individual possession like Pezulu's hat.'

'I can't help it – that's what they feel for their island. All that stuff about chancellors and cricket dances and

Nelson is because they have to back up love with legend.'

'You ethnologists dig up the most far-fetched theories.'

'Because we *do* dig, darling. I'm learning a lot from the natives.'

'The natives and the new immigrants have nothing whatever in common, Thea.'

'Mists. Slow rivers. The anthology.'

'I do wish your mother had not gone back to Africa. But that asthma of hers ...'

'Humphrey says she didn't wrap up properly.'

'What barbarous names they have!'

'Humphrey of Middlesex – it's no more comic than Tito Pezulu when one gets used to it.'

She noticed herself lingering over the name. Well, why not? You couldn't do research into a primaeval culture without perceiving and perhaps exaggerating the strange components of its charm. It was perhaps the silent world of the forest which had been disturbing her, certainly not Humphrey. The fellow was a magnificent physical specimen but he had probably never had a hot bath in all his life. About this remnant of Britons there was something unchanging – or which defied change – entirely due to the millennium of isolation. It was impossible to contrast life as it was before the Age of Destruction with the Federal life of today, and ask the question: what of any value had been preserved? A pointless question. The abolition of the nation state and its venomous patriotism had saved humanity from death after death and the real threat of extinction as suffered by so many of man's fellow animals.

'Does this Humphrey of yours love Britain in the way you tried to explain?' Pretorius asked.

'He doesn't talk about it.'

'What the devil does it matter to Silvia Brown where she lives? Industrial estates are the same everywhere.'

'She can watch the waves of the wind across the emptiness between Thames and Severn.'

'Thea, I really cannot pick up a slice of landscape and shove it in Silvia Brown's bed.'

'The only times you are ever coarse, father, is when you don't want to understand.'

'Blah! You've heard your mother say that.'

In the High Commissioner's pocket his personal receiver chirped discreetly, and he put on the head-phones. Julian Cola appeared to be reporting. Thea could only hear her father's replies.

'No, no violence! My orders are to be strictly obeyed ... Yes, I understand perfectly ... Let them talk themselves out and then shepherd them back to their estates. No arrests! ... Very well then, if you want me to see for myself relay the police cameras to my screen!'

Pretorius pushed papers to one side as the smooth top of his desk lit up and the calm shrine of sovereignty was profaned by the harsh roaring of the horde.

'The police are nervous,' Thea observed.

'I wish I could see Tito with them. He has his points at a near riot like this. Their pink and grey faces – how unpleasant they are in the mass!' Pretorius exclaimed.

'I like them when they are happy.'

'So do I – officially.'

The crowd shifted, eddying around a loud-speaker, and the roar gave place to muttering and cheering, followed by appeals for silence. A voice, clear in its cold anger, spoke from some unknown retreat.

'What do we get for good behaviour? What will they give their slaves for keeping quiet? Self-government when we are dead. Perhaps. Self-government when our children are dead. Only perhaps! But I say – NOW. Are you afraid of the Federation? Are you afraid? A hundred thousand of us against five hundred police and a gutless, idle garrison! Yes, we can deal with *them*, but what about the whole force of Euro-Africa? Well, what about it? Think! They will have to recruit men to shoot you down, to train the poor fools, transport them, drive them into the forest where we and our native brothers will wait for them in the darkness of the trees. I tell you that by the time one tenth of us have given our lives, the rest will have freedom because it is too much trouble to give them anything less.'

'Do you see much of your love in that?' Pretorius demanded bitterly above the roar of applause. 'I know that voice. A fellow calling himself Smith. The police tell me they can't identify him.'

A voice started the proscribed song, 'Landa Fope', instantly taken up by the crowd.

'That song is punishable by immediate transportation to Africa. They know it and they don't care.'

'And they don't understand half of it,' Thea added with disgust. 'It's such garbled old English. And then there's some nonsense about "Glory". A colleague of mine believes it's a sort of portmanteau word meaning to kill twice as many enemies as the number of your own men lost.'

'Damn what it means, Thea! This is serious.'

Seeing the agony which he was trying to suppress, she reached out and caught his hand.

'It shouldn't matter,' she said, trying to comfort him. 'It shouldn't.'

'Then what does? To you futile scientists, what does?'

'Truth.'

'Truth is a thing of ink and paper.'

'And of the trained observer in the field.'

'The forest. Yes. After what we've heard I'd rather you didn't go there, Thea.'

'What worries you?'

'Mounds. Those mounds of dead cities. I hate to think of oak roots underground groping to form a roof over what has no roof. And are those primitive natives so content and peaceful?'

'They have charming manners. You would feel at home with them.'

'Perhaps. But my world is this. My world is duty. I've no use for a people waiting for something in the dusk without knowing what it is or if it is. What do their manners hide, Thea?'

Chapter III

Thea was impressed as never before by the isolation of the native British, originally due to the official myth that their wilderness was radioactive: a myth cherished by both parties though no longer believed by either. She tried to assure herself that flying over blank forest on a compass course to the invisible was no more alarming than flying over the sea. The sea, too, was full of life and never a sign of it. Here, except for the darting wisps of birds, only vegetable life seemed to exist, sometimes as a lagoon of low, utterly impenetrable growth, sometimes as waves and domes of tree tops beneath which must be the two- and four-legged creatures she had come to visit.

The rare visitors from the Federation – historians, archaeologists, philologists – were usually met at the edge of the trees by their reluctant hosts, or might be permitted, if in possession of a formidable sheaf of licences, to divert one of the bantam aircraft normally used to carry mail or a distinguished passenger up from the port. It was one of these little bantams that Thea had taken, flown by the High Commissioner's personal pilot. Accustomed only to the well-marked flight path to and from the coast, he was looking anxiously around him for the narrow strip of the Middlesex landing ground, to be distinguished by stiffened red flags in the tree tops and nothing else. To Thea's relief, at last the red flags showed up against the unending green. The pilot, underestimating the length of runway, sneaked in under the great yardarm of a giant beech rather than over it. As soon as he saw Thea safely received at the end of the grass, he turned thankfully and took off like a frightened pigeon from a trap.

Humphrey and a groom were waiting with a light high-wheeled cart drawn by a pair of horned animals. The two were dressed alike in leather breeches and heavy smocks of home-spun wool with irregular patterns of green and brown. This was an unfamiliar Humphrey, for when he left the trees for Avebury he wore the plastic tunic and trousers of the ordinary immigrant, disliking, he said, to look conspicuous. He was bareheaded except for a narrow gold circlet with a small badge on the front representing an owl within a

33

wreath of leaves, and could not be mistaken for anything but a great chieftain fully conscious of his archaic world and its relationship with the Federation.

He fussed protectively over his somewhat nervous visitor, ensuring her comfort and safety on the front seat beside him. The groom handed him the reins and jumped in the back as he drove away.

'I never knew that horses could have horns,' she said. 'They don't show in the pictures of them.'

'Oh, these aren't horses, Miss Pretorius. They are racing bullocks. Much cleverer than horses in rough country. They know where to put their feet.'

Evidently the track was newly made. By its sides were the felled trees and the stacks of grass and undergrowth cleared by the scythes. Sometimes it dipped into short, steep valleys; sometimes made complicated circuits through a labyrinth of shapeless mounds and little hills, covered by elder and thorn.

'I thought the land under the trees was flat,' she said.

'It is to the north and east. But this was London.'

In her expeditions she had seen many relics of the Age of Destruction, but this grave of a great city had a sinister peace all of its own. The rainfall and fertility of Britain had shrouded the land with forest, whereas in the drier plains of the continent walls and pinnacles still stuck up from the ground like the half-buried bones of a skeleton.

The sudden noise of an animal alarmed her. So far as instinct allowed any opinion the cry was not that of a startled or ferocious creature, but neutral like the bark of a dog which could be welcoming or aggressive.

'A horse neighing,' Humphrey explained. 'We're nearly home.'

'Shall I be able to speak with your family? My Old English is not very fluent.'

'Of course. We all speak Federal. Old English is taught in the schools, but we use it only for ceremonies, festivals and incantations.'

Schools? A first example of the remarkable tribal culture. While the immigrants were attempting to revive an extinct language in the name of patriotism, speaking it badly and with a horrible accent, the forest tribes saw no object whatever in using such an inferior means of communication. Yet she found in herself a vague wish to defend the wretched efforts of immigrants from North Africa, whatever their motives, to recover something of their history and language.

'They have some bits of lost chronicles which they love and treasure,' she said.

'Do they? Well, if we are ever closer than now they can read the originals. We have an immense store of manuscripts copied and recopied.'

'Do you know what the word "Glory" means? They have a prohibited song about it called "Landa Fope".'

'It's hard to define, Miss Pretorius. We speak of the Glory of the Purpose. My brother George can explain that to you better than I. Here we are!' he added, pulling up the steaming bullocks in a flagged courtyard.

They walked in silence over the grass down an avenue of magnificent trees of which one rank suddenly opened to reveal a jumble of the red roofs of low, barn-like buildings surrounding a garden on three sides. In the centre were a sunlit pool and a fountain. On the parapet sat a lady in the flower of her age wearing a sack-like woollen garment and working the treadle of a spinning wheel with resolute energy.

Close to her, kneeling on the ground, was a fine-looking man in his middle twenties, resembling Humphrey but without his elegance. His face was burnt red by sun and wind, his fair hair needed a wash, and he was dressed in scruffy working clothes. In his hand he held a human leg bone, and was busy wiring the ankle to the shin.

Thea examined the pair of them with the delight of an ethnologist who has the luck to catch natives unawares.

'This is my mother, the Dowager of Middlesex,' Humphrey announced. 'Mamma, Miss Theodosia Pretorius, daughter of the High Commissioner.'

The Dowager got off the parapet, gave a heave to her shapeless skirt and swept an impressive court curtsey. Theodosia bowed, extended an uncertain hand and found it grasped in a hearty shake.

'And this is my brother, George.'

George put down the gruesome leg bone and greeted her like a courteous old friend. Evidently he had no use for traditional etiquette. His eyes were shamelessly admiring.

'Nothing mass-produced about this one, Humphrey,' he said. 'We'll make sure she enjoys her researches.'

The Dowager interrupted mutual compliments to yell for Guelph, who promptly appeared from the house. He was dressed much as the two brothers except that his coat was black and round his waist was a broad belt with a long sheathed knife in it.

'Bust the thread again?' he asked.

36

'It's a very delicate thread, and I'd like to see *you* spin it, Guelph! There's a capercaillie cock in the pine over there. Get your bow if it's handy!'

Guelph vanished. It was evident to Thea that the eyes of the family were following his progress through the undergrowth which hedged the garden, but she could spot neither Guelph nor the presumably dangerous creature he was ordered to exterminate. A large bird of black and green speckled with white came fluttering vainly out of the pine and crashed at her feet with an arrow through its breast. She was half shocked, half relieved.

'But why did he kill it?' she asked Humphrey.

'To eat.'

'You eat something as beautiful as that?'

'But its taste, when well hung, is as beautiful as its plumage.'

'What an original idea! I must make a note of that for the Board of Education.'

'You should. I'm all for educating them.'

'But if you have to kill things why don't you use a gun?'

George answered her:

'We do if we want a lot of game in a hurry. But the gun is very cruel. All animals hate sudden noises. It frightens them.'

'Doesn't an arrow frighten them just as much?'

'It's part of their lives. It pounces like a hawk or a wildcat. Out of silence and back to silence.'

That sinister note again! She glanced nervously at the infinities of the forest and excused her moment of uneasiness, if it should be noticed, by saying she was so used to seeing farther. It was true. This crushing vegetable life contrasted so violently with the planned landscapes of the Federation where man controlled the environment. Here the monster environment controlled man.

'George, you are frightening Miss Pretorius,' the Dowager said, 'when we all want her to feel part of us. What does your mother call you, girl?'

'Thea. All my friends do. And I wish you would.'

'What a pretty name: Thea. It just suits you,' Humphrey said.

It sounded sincere coming from that deep and sensitive voice.

'Names are so important,' she remarked in the tone proper to a scientist. 'Do the areas of forest have separate names or are they all nameless?'

'Too vast for names,' Humphrey replied, 'but some seem to have carried on through the centuries. We call this Hendon Wood. And the landing strip I made for the Federation is on hard ground which was a road. Guelph's aunt says it was named M1. You must meet her. She's a mine of traditions if you keep her mug full.'

'And what is Guelph?'

'Black Rod.'

'What does he do?'

'He speaks for the forest; and it's an old custom that he must walk backwards when he does.'

'Tradition – is that all you have of the early days when the island was abandoned?'

'That, and the manuscripts which help to form a picture of what we were. As you know, the Federation believed it had transported all the British, but it hadn't.

A remnant escaped into the wildest parts of the country and were never rounded up. Almost all were city dwellers who had always longed for a natural life and didn't realise what they were in for. There was no money and so no wages, and most died of starvation. Then somewhere – we don't know where – a settlement learned to take the few wretched animals that were still alive and to breed from them. The knowledge spread and we began to grow our own food and to get meat and clothing from cattle and sheep and to use horses to pull ploughs and turn wheels.'

'Is it true that you ride them?'

'Often.'

'Isn't it appallingly dangerous?'.

George, breaking in on Thea's history lesson, re-marked that it took courage to ride straight across country.

'George, you know very well that in our territory it can't be done at all,' said the Dowager, who had no patience with heroics. 'I expect this is all very exciting for you, Thea, but what would you like to drink?'

'Tea, please.'

'What? Tea?'

'I thought all the British drank tea.'

'You don't enjoy it, do you?'

'My father and I have to pretend we do.'

'Well, you don't have to pretend any nonsense here. Try our beer! You'll like it.'

She was sure she would not – chiefly because Tito Pezulu praised it highly and too heartily. Since he visited Humphrey of Middlesex once or twice a year on the pretext of seeing that all was well – though she was prepared to bet that he never went far from Humphrey's side – he had taken it upon himself to offer his advice before she went. He said that apart from physics and chemistry they were all a damned sight better educated than he was but warned her never to go into the darkness of the trees alone. When she asked why not, he referred obscurely to their religious beliefs. Like the usual atheists of the Federation he denied that human beings had any immaterial powers, but at the same time was afraid of them. She wondered if George had ever laced his beer with hallucinatory mushrooms.

It was Guelph who brought out the beer, pushing a keg which ran on polished wooden rollers instead of wheels. On each side, silver tankards were slotted into wooden wings upon which the grain and whorls formed a pattern as intricate as if it had been illuminated by a painter rather than by nature. Then she remembered that Guelph was no butler but spoke for the forest, whatever that meant. There was a suggestion of a time when wheels were clumsy and the only decoration was that provided by the trees themselves. Could it be that through Guelph the forest as well as the house was welcoming her?

Humphrey drew a tankard for Guelph first; then Guelph drew for him. They bowed to each other and drank. Thea asked if they were following a tradition to taste for poison.

'Yes, in a way,' Humphrey replied. 'Once upon a time, when there was only water to drink, any source could be contaminated by fallout. We are saying that we take the risk together.'

Guelph drew for the rest. Thea sipped perhaps too

cautiously, for the Dowager demanded whether the Federation allowed any alcohol at all.

'Oh, yes. It's distilled from coal and flavoured with any flower you choose. They are grown on special hot beds in the wine factories.'

'Is it possible to drink too much of it, Miss Pretorius?' Guelph asked.

'It becomes distasteful after the correct dosage.'

'And a good thing too!' George exclaimed, ignoring his mother, Humphrey and Guelph, who were all about to protest. 'And that reminds me. How's old Sam's knee this morning, Guelph?'

'Bust not bruised, if you ask me.'

'Not good for him, parties at his age! Woke up in the straw. Tried to wipe his filthy beard with the cow's tail and got kicked. Well, I'd better have another look at it.'

George picked up the leg bone and waved it cheerfully at Thea by way of farewell.

'But we should have this poor man flown out,' she implored, overcome by the white and wagging bone and forgetting that the only means of calling up a bantam craft from Avebury was by at least three days of arduous travel. 'Has George studied medicine?'

'Enough for us and the animals. And there's nothing like a small stable for learning the proper bedside manner,' the Dowager assured her. 'Lord bless us, I don't see how you Euro-Africans stay alive at all when you get all hot and bothered about a stiff knee and grow your liquor on a manure heap!'

'I know yours is made by the old – the senior women of the tribe,' Thea said nervously.

'Who the devil told you that?'

41

'It's in Schröder's *Manners and Customs of the Native English*.'

'Ass! I remember that fellow. Came here soon after the island was opened up and spent his time asking about pre-marital relationships. Just got engaged, I had, and you know, Humphrey, how that sort of thing embarrassed your poor father. He couldn't even spit out what he wanted in plain language. Pre-marital relationships, indeed! The only one he ever got was with Black Rod's aunt, moustache and all, and what did she tell us about that, Guelph?'

'It was a little beyond me, Dowager. It appeared that the usual roles were reversed.'

Humphrey, fearing his mother's further reminiscences, waved to the side door of the house as if answering an appeal.

'I think cook wants to speak to you, mamma.'

'Dam' fellow always thinks he knows more than I do till he's halfway through. Grub, Miss Thea, grub! That's what's made by the old women of the tribe. Pah!'

She marched off in dignified fury. Guelph followed with a nod to Humphrey indicating that he was prepared to act as lightning conductor.

'I am so sorry I have offended her,' Thea said.

'You can't offend the wind. Let it blow and be refreshed by it.'

She took the Dowager's place on the low wall of the pool, played with the spinning wheel and sipped her beer. Humphrey was standing over her, and she lifted her head to hold his eyes before returning more primly to her notebook.

'I think I like your beer.'

42

'Yes, it grows on you. I get it from a little tribe in Kent.'

'Do you use money to pay for it?'

'No, a credit at our trading centres. They are very like your banks.'

'But since yours is the richest tribe, how do you prevent all the rest being in debt to you?'

'I just raise the value of what they have to sell until the account balances. Take this beer, now: since its quality is unique, its value is what I choose to pay for it, and no less.'

'Less? Can you do what you like, then?'

'Within reason. I tell my people what to make, and they see that it is made. They tell me what to plant and I see that is planted.'

'But that is like the ancient feudal system.'

'Is it? Pezulu Pasha said it was communism. Names aren't so important as you think, Thea. If you give a system a name, people feel they ought to live up to it. But there can be orderly systems with no name. What about the twists and turns of a flight of starlings?'

'But then it's all instinctive,' she replied, impatiently closing her notebook. 'Don't we have anything but a language in common?'

'You and I?'

It was not, she felt, an occasion for another meeting of eyes with this fascinating barbarian.

'You and the High Commissioner for example.'

'Oh – er – mutual respect.'

Her father had asked, rather emotionally, what lay behind their manners. This might be an opportunity, if not too early, to find out.

'Would you be on his side if the new immigrants revolted?'

'Revolt? Them?'

'But you know almost nothing of them. Since the Age of Destruction you and they have developed differently as two new species.'

That was true. But how wrong it had been to think of the forest British as a mere primitive tribe! Together with the men and women of courage and character seven hundred years ago who had created a viable agricultural society, they had another sort of wealth to be exploited: the remains of the libraries and the tales and manuscripts of those early heroes. Forgotten and left to themselves to die out, they owed nothing to the Federation but a common language recently acquired. Schröder, the missionary and explorer, had written that they were like the Romanised Britons who had adopted the language of the conquerors, but he was wrong. There had never been any conqueror, only a trickle of visitors from the mainland in the last hundred years. Those, however, had been enough for a people of astonishing vision to foresee a future when they, too, would inevitably be a part of the Federation; and so they had deliberately and by common consent – what a meeting of the chieftains there must have been! – chosen to teach themselves and their children to become bilingual.

'Yet any of you could be licenced to live in the Federation if you wished,' she said.

'We should be unhappy anywhere but here.'

'But you have such a lack of comfort living always in the darkness of the trees and the smell of the earth and the mist.'

'There is a chalk stream running fast through the hazels. I must show you that when the mist lifts after sunrise.'

'And what about streams which vanish and the fear of what may be underground?'

'Why fear? Underground are just rats and otters.'

'They never come out?'

'Only for George.'

'But if you so love the place you should understand the immigrants' patriotism.'

'I hate that futile patriotism!' – he rose gracefully to his feet, growing from the wellhead, 'Look, Thea, I stand here. So does the tree. On any other earth we couldn't.'

'It would not matter to me what earth I stood on.'

'I am so glad of that.'

She revised her too casual statement in near panic:

'I meant just that I am rootless.'

'I am the roots.'

Chapter IV

Alfred Brown was quite ignorant that his house had been used as a secret rendezvous for leaders of the British freedom fighters. It had been Silvia who had offered it to them. She knew exactly the hours when her father would be engaged in public duties and her mother – whose simple morning was unchangeable – would be at the shops, to be followed by a visit to the Community Association for a restoring cup of tea. Silvia then had the house to herself and, being the respectable home of a member of the Assembly, it was most unlikely to be suspected.

In that living room where the assassination of the High Commissioner had been plotted, Smith and Green again sat in conference, accompanied now by the Chancellor of the Exchequer. There was no reason why they should not come openly as passive members of Silvia's party to sympathise and discuss the future. Brown himself, repelled, powerless, forlorn, left them in that once peaceful room of fake antiques, deliberately avoiding controversy.

Among the immigrants public opinion was divided. After Smith's inflammatory speeches and the singing of 'Landa Fope', there had been no arrests. The wise tolerance of Ali Pretorius had paid off. Avebury was a little ashamed of its mob hysteria.

Smith thumped the table. He never had more than one gesture: to raise his fist above his head and bring it down again.

'Provocation! That's what I need. Provocation before the people go off the boil.'

Green remarked that Pretorius would be careful not to give any, that he had been frightened out of his life.

'Frightened? Pretorius hasn't an emotion in him, only a smirk on his mongrel face! There's no trick he won't stoop to – even mercy.'

'In my humble opinion, Pezulu will ...' Green began.

'Pezulu will play right into our hands. There's nothing he and I would like more than a dozen British corpses.'

The Chancellor had sat in silent meditation, piously absorbed in the contemplation of his finger nails.

'If only they knew all,' he said softly. 'If only they knew.'

Green protested that ten thousand of his leaflets had been distributed the day before.

'And what's the good of them?' Smith replied. 'It's time you intellectuals learnt practical politics. People can't be warmed into revolt. They must be thrown into the flames before they see them.'

There was a knock at the door. Mrs Brown opened it to ask if the three visitors would like their tea now. She looked at them with a landlady's stolid disapproval of, say, a noisy drunk who at the same time pays his rent regularly. The three faces were so different from those of her friends, genial in their simplicity and round as herself. She suspected that they might be leaders of the gang which had corrupted her Silvia, but perhaps now they could help.

She had been pressed by husband and daughter to join the British immigrants from Africa, but the move was all against her instinct for security and comfort. Everything in Britain was foreign. She had always been nervous about the strange people hidden in the forest, imagining that a hairy man might sneak out and kidnap her Silvia. She was equally disturbed by these dissidents who were not content with the peaceful, pleasant life within the Federation and were responsible for the childish propaganda which had inspired her daughter to shoot at that nice man, Ali Pretorius.

The fellow called Green rushed at her and put an unwelcome arm round her shoulders.

'The true, heroic British mother!' he cried. 'Silvia's sacrifice shall not be in vain. It shall echo round the world. Leave it to me, dear, broken-hearted Mrs Brown.'

While Green detained her with prattle and pawings, Smith whispered quickly to the Chancellor.

'That story of yours – stretch it a bit! It doesn't matter how. Get him all excited about what he's going to write and he'll believe it himself.'

Green closed the door behind Mrs Brown, still speaking of the martyrdom of Silvia. The Chancellor watched his gesticulations with interest; they were at least more tolerable than those of Smith, and should be noted for future use in any sentimental context.

'Pretorius hasn't made her a martyr yet,' Smith said.

'If only they knew!' the Chancellor repeated. 'If only they knew!'

'Knew what?'

'My lambs, I have had time to consider my duty. Am I to tell the truth or not? Alas, the incalculable effects! And yet to have seen the child helpless before those brutes!'

'What *is* this? Green demanded. 'Why haven't I heard of it? Are my cell and I distrusted?'

'Never! We should lose our way without your steadfast liberal minds. Chancellor, what, for God's sake, did you see?'

'They told her in my presence that they would soon cure her by doing to her what her husband would and threatened her with a rope. I could not tell whether they meant death or worse.'

'Speak out, man!' Smith charged him. 'We're not children.'

'She was laid on the floor with her defenceless legs apart.'

'And then?'

'I could bear no more. I left. When I was outside I heard her screams. They still echo in my ears.'

Smith, seeing that his partner was not quite as impressed as he should have been, buried his face in his hands.

'I know we cannot expect you intellectuals to feel as we do,' he said. 'We have never had your advantages, you see.'

'Damn you, Smith! I am a man of the people, and what they feel, I feel.'

'Then tell them what they feel!'

'I shall publish this atrocity fearlessly.'

Mrs Brown returned with tea and a glowering husband. Alfred was a sturdy man in his middle forties, his tunic forming a slope above his too generous belly, but well framed in muscle. Though not a member of the first immigration, and as a speaker more forthright than eloquent, he had been elected to the Assembly with a comfortable majority.

His greying hair and – normally – kindly smile proclaimed a character of competence and responsibility who would give his best to any cause in which he believed; but few realised what that 'best' was. It included a touch of youth and adventure which had carried his family to Britain, but since then had been unused for want of a society that could use it.

'My lamb! My dear lamb!' the Chancellor bleated.

'Cut it out, cock! What I say is that it's a dirty trick to use my house just because I'm above suspicion.

You may have been at it for months for all I know.'

'You will obey the action committee,' Smith said.

'All right! All right! I'm aware of it. You've outvoted your own executive and we can take it. You needn't rub it in. What about my daughter?'

'The people will free your daughter,' Green trumpeted, 'with their bare hands, if need be.'

'Don't talk bloody nonsense, mate! Is she all right, Smith?'

'All right? After that? Ask your Chancellor!'

'I left before it happened. I saw nothing.'

'But he heard her screams,' Smith added.

'Always did when she couldn't have her way.'

'How can you say such a thing, Alfred?' Mrs Brown reproached him.

'Pezulu tied her down and raped her.'

'In front of Pretorius? Stuff that for a yarn!'

'My little Silvia! My little Silvia!' Mrs Brown sobbed.

'Now, now, mother! Have a bit of common sense!'

'You call the Chancellor a liar?' Smith demanded.

'Wouldn't dream of it! But fact is fact. And politics is politics.'

On the streets of Avebury, since distances were short and walking recommended for the health of the citizens, the only motorised transport was that of the police, ambulance and fire services; thus the engine which whispered up Alfred Brown's street and stopped outside his house could only be that of a police car. Smith and Green had long been prepared for such an emergency. They dashed to the outer wall, pulled up two floor-boards which had been lightly tacked down, and extracted two official caps and overalls with a bag of tools. By the time the Federal Police were knocking at the door, they had a loop of cable in their hands and had become anonymous servants of communal anonymity.

'I'm coming!' Mrs Brown called, stifling her sobs. 'I'm coming! Mind the paint!'

She let in an Inspector followed by a municipal police officer carrying an instrument case.

The Chancellor, who had not moved from his seat, asked:

'Would you intrude upon a family's grief?'

'I'm sorry, your Worship. I'm sure Mr Brown will believe I'm not here from choice, knowing him personally as it were,' the policeman said.

'That's all right, mate,' Alfred assured him. 'Orders is orders.'

The Inspector asked Smith and Green what they were up to.

'Avebury Power Board. There's a short down here somewhere.'

'Well, get out!'

'Have to come back this evening if we do.'

Green added a nice touch by grumbling obscurely:

'Always something! If it ain't children, it's drains. And if it ain't drains, it's the police.'

They put back the boards, tapped them with a hammer and cleared out with their bag of tools, caps well down over their faces.

The Chancellor asked if he, too, was to leave.

'As you please,' the Inspector replied. 'But it's my duty to report your presence here.'

'His Excellency can only approve. He would expect me to be at *my* post as I expect him to be at his.'

The Chancellor gathered his black frock coat together with dignity, bowed deeply to Mrs Brown and left.

'Stately old sod, isn't he,' the policeman remarked.

'You've no right to speak like that of the Chancellor of the Exchequer!'

'I take it back, Mr Brown. I only meant that I see what you see in him, if you see what I mean.'

The Inspector held out a document to Alfred Brown, requesting him to satisfy himself that the search warrant was in order.

'You have no right. I am a member of the Assembly.'

'Only a formality, Mr Brown. Pezulu Pasha knows that you are opposed to violence.'

'Aye, it never settled nothing. Nor does patience, more's the pity. That's what the young ones like Silvia see.'

The Inspector opened the case carried by his companion, and placed on the table an advanced metal detector with horizontal revolving vanes. Whenever the vanes stopped, a pointer sprang out from the body of the machine. The Inspector ignored the obvious metal objects indicated, but showed interest when the pointer reacted to the wooden case of the grandfather clock.

'What's that thing for?' he asked.

'To look handsome. That's all. Some say it was to tell the time.'

Mrs Brown, feeling that her husband had been too blunt, explained that it was a piece of old British woodwork.

'Alfred brought it with us from Africa. And it's valuable, see?'

'Where does it open?'

'It don't open,' Alfred said. 'And there's nothing in it so far as I know.'

'Stand clear of the beam, please.'

The Inspector threw a switch and the fine beam of a laser cut its path round the front of the clock, which fell on the floor to reveal an old-fashioned rifle in a rack.

'This is your daughter's, of course?'

The two Browns stared at each other, appalled at the probable consequences. After a moment's hesitation, Alfred Brown replied:

'Mine.'

'It's of the same make and pattern as her weapon, and there was another here very recently.'

'Aye. She must have got in through the top and taken one. That's what put it in her head. Impulse, like. Like when a child gets hold of a box of matches. Got to light one, hasn't she?'

'Come off it, Brown. We know she's a member of the terrorist group.'

'Well, you know wrong! *We* wouldn't trust her. She's just a young fool. Hysterical!'

The policeman, much shocked, declared he would never have believed it of Mr Brown.

'You don't know what it is to be British, lad.'

'If I had my way,' the Inspector said, 'I'd kick all you bastards into the forest and see how you liked that!'

'They ain't British. It's we who are the British. Down with the Federation!'

'Pack a bag, Brown – change of underclothes, toothbrush and anything else private and personal. We'll provide the rest.'

'Oh, not both of you!' Mrs Brown cried. 'Not both of you!'

Chapter V

Cold steel. Pretorius did not fear it, but shuddered away from the mental picture of one human being cutting and stabbing another. When the sun shone on individuals in the small bands of insurgents which picketed the streets leading to the Residency, some object between belt and thigh occasionally flashed. Cold steel.

They had firearms too, but not many. The Sporting Club armouries must have been raided. Distant cheering and the singing of 'Landa Fope' could be heard from the direction of the Assembly, but the pickets were silent – a bad sign. Old histories recorded that the British were most dangerous when they were grimly silent.

Suddenly there came the sound of a shot from somewhere close to, probably one of the gates of the Residency compound. Pretorius jumped up, shouting involuntarily:

'Stop it! Stop it, I tell you!'

The shot was followed by a roar of anger, almost immediately succeeded by jeers and laughter. Contempt? Contempt just as if the nearest picket had heard his futile order? But that was impossible when he was at his desk trying, not very successfully, to dictate to Julian Cola the headings of a confidential report.

'Julian, go down and identify that man who fired against my orders and put him under arrest!'

Pezulu Pasha, having heard the shot, hurried to the High Commissioner's office in order – as he said to himself – to put some guts into him.

'Well, they asked for it that time. One of them crept up and catapulted a bad egg at the sentry, who thought they were going to try to rush the gate.'

'Which of your men was fool enough to fire?'

'Not one of mine, sir. Army.'

'Julian, get me Lieutenant General Aranda. Tito, was this a serious attack?'

'Not yet. But they are threatening everything, and we can't tell where the real strike will come.'

'They have a right to protest. I have jailed a member of their Assembly.'

'But he was guilty as hell.'

'Of what? Of producing a daughter?'

'And of bringing her up on their filthy patriotism and running an arms depot for her boy friends.'

'I will not form my policy on impatience.'

'Patience can't go on for ever, sir.'

'Why not?'

'Because one can't govern a madhouse.'

'Doctors do.'

'They couldn't if they had no force behind them.'

'The Federation has overwhelming force. That's why I don't have to use it.'

Yes, overwhelming force in principle and by agreement between all three Federations. The Americans, always the most idealistic of the three, had abolished their armed forces entirely. Pretorius approved but had to admit that they had ruthlessly strengthened the powers of civil police. The Asian Federation, unwilling to lose the pictured splendour and pageantry of the past, had kept small garrisons purely for ceremonial. The Euro-Africans had done much the same but, since they had pockets of disaffection and organised crime among frontier peoples who had never suffered the worst effects of the Age of Destruction and did not wholly appreciate the lessons which the rest had learned for ever, had preserved a General Staff chiefly to evaluate the limits of minimum force, allowing enough troops to keep them happy.

General Arpad Aranda, immaculately uniformed, strode through the double door and saluted. He had the air of cheerful confidence proper to the traditional soldier, especially when uncertain what to be confident about. He carried a rolled-up map under his left arm and a briefcase in the hand.

'General Aranda, any man who fires is to be put under arrest immediately.'

'Naturally, sir. The shot which disturbed us all was let off by a guardsman who had not been trained in the use of old-fashioned firearms which are all the Federation will permit us. He mistook the function of the trigger.'

'I trust he has been removed from his post.'

'Yes, sir. To hospital.'

'Are the Residency guards really in any serious trouble at all?'

'That will depend on your orders, sir.'

Pezulu interrupted excitedly that his police, too, were waiting for orders.

'Suppose they are attacked and the High Commissioner has still not declared a State of Emergency?'

'One cannot expect a decision from His Excellency until he is in possession of the facts.'

The intolerable military! Pretorius hated the coolness of this admirable servant as he hung upon the wall a map of Avebury, unfastened his briefcase and selected three coloured chalks. All his movements were unhurried and meticulous. For all the emotion he showed, Aranda might have been arranging the seating for a state banquet. Meanwhile the angry roar of the crowd from the parks and playgrounds around the Institute was drawing nearer, or else increasing in mindless ferocity. Didn't it worry the man that what he was about to arrange was indeed seating but for coffins?

Aranda circled with chalk a point in the centre of the city.

'The position at fifteen hours forty-seven was that all police had been withdrawn from the welfare estates.'

Pezulu's nerves were affected as much as the High Commissioner's by this professional composure.

'I'm not going to have 'em murdered,' he half shouted.

'Quite so! Quite, Pezulu Pasha! But I am here to give His Excellency my appreciation of the situation as it is, not as it might be. The insurgents, numbering twenty to twenty-two thousand, may move so' – Aranda dashed a red arrow across the map, marking it 'A' – 'or so;' – he drew a blue arrow and marked it 'B' – 'I cannot tell the intentions of the enemy – I beg your pardon, sir, the British – until they have committed themselves. If their objective is "A", the barracks are isolated. I cannot reinforce without bloodshed and I can only order my Area Commander to surrender.'

'Why must he?'

'Because if he is not allowed to fire and must meet cold steel with truncheons and riot shields, his position will be overrun. Passing now to "B", the threat is to the Residency and Administration Offices. I take it that it will be your wish that they should be defended if attacked?'

'Of course it is!'

'I am merely giving you an analysis of the situation, sir,' Aranda replied, overlooking the High Commissioner's impatience. 'There are two alternatives open to us. One is to surrender "B" and fly a mobile column from Federation Headquarters into the heart of the city while the insurgents are unprepared and dispersed.'

He permitted himself a single sweeping gesture which seemed to scoop the column from Pretorius' desk, launch it across the Channel and deposit it in Avebury.

'The second alternative is to form a stronghold at "B" and allow it to be invested. That will inevitably involve the use of fire-arms which, as I have mentioned, are obsolete and not markedly superior to those in the hands of the British, but we have enough of them for defence.'

'And if I authorise you to use ... to use ...'

'The so-called beeswarm, sir?'

'What exactly is the beeswarm, Aranda?'

'It was once known as grapeshot, sir, and is delivered by quick-firing cannon with a much wider spread of shot than was known to the armies of the Age of Destruction. They would probably have used nerve gas.'

'Revolting! But I have heard that there is now a more merciful weapon which can be programmed to pick out the ringleaders.'

'Nowhere near it yet, sir. The scientists say it can't be done without silicon chips, and all they are sure of is that a vein of the stuff existed somewhere on the Pacific coast of North America. But the desert climate there is so cruel, with the few inhabitants reduced to hunter-gatherers, that all records are lost.'

'Thank you, General. You have covered very ably the military problems.'

Pretorius rose from his desk and strode across to the map.

'We will now deal with the political. Our dislike of the British! Our ignorance! Our intolerance!'

With each accusation he slashed an arrow across the map, and stood back glaring.

'I agree, sir. But the British have those unpleasant qualities too.'

Aranda, unruffled, had spoken with his practised military manners, recalling Pretorius, still appalled at the thought of turning beeswarm on his nursery school, to his normal courtesy.

'I am so sorry, Aranda. They do, of course.'

'And I did warn you this could happen,' Pezulu said.

'You're always warning me. What particular occasion was this?'

'Your personal interview with Silvia Brown.'

'And what the devil was wrong with that? It was my duty to be as gentle as I could with the poor girl.'

'It's said that you tied her down.'

'What for?'

'With her legs apart.'

'And raped her, I suppose,' Pretorius added incredulously.

'No. I did that. They have the word of the Chancellor of the Exchequer for it.'

'The Chancellor? But why should I have invited him to watch something so loathsome?'

'So that he could report back to his precious lambs how the Federation settles with assassins. It's all in this morning's underground sheet.'

'Who wrote it?'

'According to a very reliable source, a fellow called Green.'

'Have him arrested at once!'

'We did. Wrong man.'

'Can't you identify him?'

'They all live in similar houses. Most of them are called White, Green, Brown or Black. They all work from nine to one, and watch the screen from three to midnight ...'

Aranda remarked cheerfully that the more civilisation progressed, the harder it was for the police to identify anybody. Pretorius, having no use for generalities from the mess, ignored him and demanded what the Chancellor had to say for himself.

'Says he is appalled. Says the report misquotes him. Says everything except that his story is a damned lie. So it's not surprising they believe it.'

'Not surprising when they know me? When every week for two years I've mixed with them in their streets and houses alone and unguarded? One tries to have every sympathy with them, but how can one describe such stupidity?'

'British,' Pezulu answered.

'What *are* the British? A race or a religion or just a mob with coloured hair and the habit of rotting their brains with that dismal liquid they call tea? God knows I did not mind being shot at, but ...'

'The poor girl?' Pezulu murmured.

'I don't see why you call her poor. She's a terrorist like her father and his whole group.'

'Don't take it to heart, sir. They were dead certain you wouldn't strike back.'

'Were they, by God!'

Pezulu cautiously remarked – as if it were a mere possibility – that declaring a State of Emergency needn't necessarily ...

'I'll sign that at once. And Silvia Brown?'

'I know you feel strongly that we should not give any provocation.'

'Provocation, Tito, is not the same thing as restoring order.'

'Then let justice be seen to be done.'

'Immediate deportation for trial on a charge of nationalism?'

'She wanted to be St Silvia the martyr, I remember. Make it first-degree criminal patriotism.'

Pretorius gathered up the papers from his desk, wrote and stamped the single sheet remaining, and then signed it so heavily that the ink sputtered.

'General Aranda, if attacked you may use firearms. If their use is not sufficient to hold both "A" and "B", here is your authorisation to employ the beeswarm with a due regard for economy.'

He rose and left the office with the walk of a strong and silent man.

'If only he handles this confidently!' declared Pezulu, punching his wounded hat with excitement.

Aranda calmly rolled up his map.

'I must write this up for the staff course,' he said. 'We Euro-Africans have so little experience of sheer courage. I suppose the sight of their own dead will stop them?'

'No it won't! Not if I know the British!'

Aranda's forecast of the fate of 'A' was correct. The British attack on the barracks went home. The troops, untrained or poorly trained to use their ceremonial rifles for killing, escaped from the thrust of the charge, from the stones, the clubs and the red knives that no longer shone in the sun, by rushing into the empty streets and the groves of the parks, tearing off their uniform tunics.

The Area Commander, trying desperately to remember all he had learned in school of the ancient and dignified rituals of surrender, marched forward with a white flag. Two improvised swords of sharpened iron bars met in his chest and the killers, to their surprise, found some difficulty in withdrawing them.

The British casualties were insignificant, mostly caused by the crushing and treading of their own undisciplined mass. War – if this was war – seemed to them a much easier business than the annihilation of whole populations, of cities and even of the fertility of the earth which had led to the lasting peace of the World Federations. Confident and jeering, they turned now to that seat of power and integrity which Aranda had so comprehensively included under the letter 'B'.

The Residency and the government offices formed a roughly oval compound set on the smooth green hillock a little above the city. It was not encircled by any wall or railing, but the ranks of windows on the east side were unbroken and gave an impression of bureaucratic solidity; on the west side were three gateways, the central one formal and classical, the other two no more than arched entrances. Stretching along the whole west front was a wide, paved terrace at the head of the two avenues from the city.

Theodosia Pretorius watched the horde of stormers which smothered the green of the slope. Instead of turning the field of battle dark, the pale colours of normal, everyday tunics made it iridescent as the onrushing foam of a broken wave. She was appalled to see a sprinkling of women among the men. But why not? It could not be assumed that Silvia Brown was the only one who valued bloodstained patriotism above peace and prosperity.

She became aware that she was very much alone at her west window. The secretariat, seeing that there was no hope of the attack being repulsed by the sentries at the main gate or any available reinforcements, had now fled across to the east wing where they hoped at least for mercy. Curiosity – human or professional – had held her where she was. Her father had retired to his private suite, where he could weep without witnesses. Tito Pezulu had sneaked in time down to the town where, by now unrecognisable, he was probably hidden away among his secret agents. The only other authority who could advise her what to do, that absurd soldier Aranda, was buzzing about the interior courtyard and garden, no doubt shouting orders to which nobody would give any attention.

She crossed the room and looked out into the courtyard. Aranda was indeed buzzing about and shouting orders. With a handful of men he had blocked the main gate with a curious machine not unlike the wide mouth of a dragon set with tubes instead of teeth, and was supervising the loading of racks of ammunition into its grey belly. Whatever it was, it had been driven into position just in time. The wave of insurgents had already engulfed the terrace.

As she was crossing the room back to her former position she heard the roar of the discharge and involuntarily ducked. It was a rippling roar, perhaps resembling the chatter of machine guns of which one read in histories of war, or the spaced explosion of tactical atomic bombs laying waste their

66

colossal avenues of death immediate or death deferred.

The view from the west window had utterly changed. There was plenty of green now to be seen on the slope and tiny rivulets of red were seeking the edge of the terrace. Here and there men still stood upright, isolated and unwounded, among others who lay still or crawled or wriggled. Those who could run ran back and reformed in the dead ground halfway down the slope. She could distinguish the formation of groups and their leaders. The obvious course was to split into columns and take one of the two undefended gates by flank attack. They tried. The sight of their own dead did not stop them. But meanwhile the dragon had boldly emerged into the open. So far as she could tell not one of the British got further than the terrace.

The green gap between defenders and attackers was now silent or, rather, gave an impression of silence in spite of the groans and cries of the wounded which formed a background like the loud chattering of birds in the silence of dawn. From the front ranks of the British a single woman strode out dressed in white and leading a child by the hand. She had no need of speech or gestures; the meaning of her steady advance to death was plain to everyone. It was not an offer of surrender, nor any heroic attempt to restore the morale of the defeated. It was protest.

On and on the two walked until they reached the terrace, the white-clad woman upright as a statue, the child trusting its mother to lead it safely through this adult hell. One man of the many thousands responded to her unspoken message: the soldier who had killed from duty, not from hate, the soldier trained to accept the cost of the guilt he must conceal. Aranda paced out from the gate and saluted her. He then lifted her hand, stood for a moment by her side facing the half-formed columns of the attack, and led her back onto the grass.

Below them, into that deadly gap where spiritual courage had made a space for peace, ventured the first ambulances and stretcher-bearers weeping and vomiting, helpless from lack of experience, but taking advantage of the silence and hesitation of the adversaries. It was the end.

Chapter VI

After three intolerable days of withdrawal into a divided self, Thea had sought assurance from the neutral forest: not for physical safety, since the Residency was no longer in any danger, but safety for her opinions and personality. The courage of those British immigrants had deeply impressed her, let alone the still greater courage of that unknown woman who had stopped the massacre by the offer of herself and her child. And why and how had the professional soldier

69

instantly understood her gesture, this Arpad Aranda whom she had always pictured as a cold representative of the outdated 'art' of war and quite unmoved by the inhumanity of it.

Were nationalism and its attendant patriotism such deadly crimes? Well, of course they were. Yet there remained in her mind the splendour of willingness to die for such follies. All she had been brought up to believe and did believe was for the moment in question. Her father could be of no help; his ideals were fixed and unshakeable, and she would not have him any different. Humphrey of Middlesex, however, with his humour and his curious grasp of essentials might restore her equanimity. Within his tribe and his family the problem of nationalism and patriotism were unknown and unneeded.

She told her father where she would be. As always he disapproved but did accept that his Thea's emotions were overwhelmed and that if she chose to continue her researches in the forest that might be as healthy for her as a return to Africa. He sent with her an escort of four armed police with orders – on her insistence – to leave her as soon as she entered the forbidden territory. No police were necessary. When she left Avebury streets were empty and houses were shut to keep out the dawn.

She sat down on a fallen trunk much farther into the wilderness than even the most adventurous child had ever dared to go. How and by whom her presence would be noticed she could not know, but she was certain that it would be. Humphrey's need of up-to-date intelligence from the outer world meant that someone unseen and unsuspected would be watching the open ground of Avebury.

She was in a temple of the trees; nothing but their pillars held up the sky, a sky which stayed invisible except in patches where bramble and tall bracken could find a way to the sun. It was not from this ground cover that George of Middlesex appeared, but from the mass of trunks where a man, still and upright as they, could glide from one to another to reach his objective.

'All quiet?' he asked.

'Except in their hearts and ours.'

'No more Landa Fope?'

'I liked the tune.'

'Perhaps that is all that matters. Well, I've sent back a runner with the good news of your arrival. We'll have to walk an hour and a bit till we pick up my tandem. Horses this time, Thea! None of Humphrey's grunting bullocks.'

The path twisted between tree trunks over the dead leaves and more directly through the patches of under-growth where George led the way, slashing down branches of thorn and drooping nettles which might have touched her. After an hour of easy walking they came out into an open glade where two slender ponies were grazing. Near them was a curious vehicle with two large, light wheels between which the driver sat. Behind it was a two-wheeled trailer covered by a thick mattress.

'My emergency ambulance, Thea. I take it whenever I want to get a patient – or sometimes myself – away quickly.'

Seeing that she kept a careful distance from the ponies, he told her to touch them.

'Stroke their noses and pat their necks. They enjoy attention just like you and I.'

Nervously she did so, and found that the bite she expected turned out to resemble a kiss.

'How did they survive the cold and darkness and poisonous grass?' she asked.

While he harnessed the two ponies to the trap, one in front of the other, George answered her with a story of the far past.

'By Love,' he said. 'There was a dying stallion on the downs, perhaps not far from Avebury, and with him his dying trainer. The trainer was never very clear how he came to clean food and water. He swore that a passer-by had led them to a barn but he saw no more of the man and would sometimes say that he had dreamed him. However, he cherished and fed his stallion till it could walk firmly and he himself ate whatever he could find in the burnt villages of the deserted land. They walked side by side to the west and there he met another like himself who loved his beasts and had kept alive the two last mares of the little moorland breed. It was he who wrote down the story for us as best he could. Together they helped the stallion to cover the mares, believing that must be the purpose of the dream, if it was a dream. Soon afterwards the stallion died and with him his trainer having nothing more to give to life. But from the mares came a colt and a filly and from them all our horses are descended.'

When the pair of ponies were ready in their traces he placed Thea in the trailer on her back and strapped her in.

'You're going to bump up and down a bit,' he told

her, 'but that won't bother you. There's a foot of goose feathers between you and the floor. Give me a yell if you feel sick and we'll take it much slower.'

He mounted to the box and the tandem trotted neatly away. The path was sometimes a ribbon of grass under a patchwork of leaves, sometimes a tunnel under branches, and always so narrow that it would be possible for one man to keep miles of it in perfect condition. That, she supposed, was why this vehicle itself was so very narrow. The bumps neither threw George off his seat nor her off her goose feathers, but the journey to the east reminded her of being tossed in a blanket for fun when she was a child. Though neither bruised nor seasick she was thankful when George unstrapped her and set her on her feet.

So there were inns, too, in this land. A low house stood in a clearing with its garden running down to a leisurely river. At the beat of the tireless little hooves, a woman came out and greeted George with a delight in which there was no shade of deference. She was tall with the gracious slimness of age, grey hair loose on her shoulders and dressed in a jerkin and skirt of supple leather.

'Got a room for the lady?' George asked.

'If she don't mind the barn owl. I'll tell him to stop his snoring.'

'Give him a fat mouse with my compliments when he comes home. And what have you for her?'

'Trout tonight and beauties, Mr George.'

'Ha! Miss Pretorius is in luck.'

'Pretorius? I've heard that name somewhere. Devon, maybe?'

Neither of them commented. Thea, noticing that the

73

landlady spoke poor Federal, switched the conversation to Old English. Avebury and the whole damned Federation were blessedly far away.

'Now I must leave you,' George said, 'but you needn't have a care in the world. If I pick you up early we shall reach Humphrey in the late afternoon.'

'You have patients here?'

'Yes. One who has a cough I don't like, but we must all die sometime; another who will be fit again if he surrenders himself as I tell him to the wind in the rushes. And there is a tree, the tallest oak, it is said, in all Britain, to whose life I must pray, giving thanks for my horses and, such as they are, for my gifts.'

'I thought you were all atheists. That's what Schröder says.'

'He did not understand. We are animists. We give thanks to the purpose wherever its Glory is manifest – in the egg which carries the colours of a butterfly, in the seed which contains the shape and destiny of an oak, in a universe which obeys its own laws. Your scientists know the how but neither we nor they know the why. I think that scientists never did, even before the Age of Destruction. Yet the why is there and the spirits who are not blinded by material can sometimes give the answer.'

'Can you see them?' she asked, vaguely thinking of Pezulu and his warnings of the night.

'That depends on who looks and gives them praise.'

Her room was simple and spotless, lit when the forest swallowed the sun by a large candle with the incense smell of resin. Except for the candle and the owl it might have been anywhere in the remoter provinces of the Federation. The owl's quarters consisted of a long, dark box at ceiling level, the entrance outside and on the inside a grating which allowed conversation, if desired, with any fellow occupant of the room.

The owl was preening plumage before leaving for the evening; with enormous eyes he observed Thea and the landlady who presented him with a dead mouse, still warm, with the compliments of George, and requested him not to snore when he returned home. Thea could have sworn there was a change in the luminous eyes at the mention of George.

'Does he understand what you say to him?' she asked.

'Well, as he don't answer back I don't know. But Mr George and he don't need words. He's a very reverent owl, Mr George says.'

Thea approached her grilled trout with caution, for the only fish familiar to her were the federally approved fingers sometimes modelled of fish paste to resemble the living creature. Daringly she asked for a glass of beer, and sat over her meal trying to make sense of George as apparently a doctor of men and a priest of animals, a very different character from the enchantingly regal Humphrey. But even Humphrey, she remembered, when she asked him the meaning of the Old English word 'Glory', had spoken mysteriously of the Glory of the Purpose.

She went to bed early, feeling slightly pulped in spite of the merciful goose feathers. The owl woke her up when he landed heavily in their common home. She dozed off again to the rhythm of his snoring – for he did snore – annoyed with her imagination for sleepily insisting that he was repeating over and over again the first syllable of 'Humphrey'.

She was already up and in the riverside garden when dawn greeted her. Greeted was the right word. In the cities of the Federation, dawn did not greet; it arrived in a business-like manner, welcome or not. Here the birds, the plopping of the fish, the unfolding of the buds resumed the Purpose of the day. She found herself using in thought the brothers' name for God. Like most Euro-Africans she had no religious beliefs. But it did occur to her that if communion with nature had continued undisturbed for seven hundred years, a personal name for that Unity was not needed and atheism meaningless.

George and his tandem trotted out of the forest. The owl drifted from its bedroom and silently swung twice above them while the ponies' heads followed the white ghost with companionable interest. She was strapped on to the trailer again, mildly complaining. All the same, she had begun to be fascinated by the curious viewpoint of the track that had been passed rather than the track ahead, of the exuberance of vegetation above her rather than the long vista of crowded trunks through which the ponies must wind their way.

On their arrival after the long day she was resurrected to a splendour of welcome and carried off by the Dowager, indignant at George's method of transport, to the guest room prepared for her, to rest and a bath. In spite of the primitive resources of this haunting palace, her mother, she thought, could hardly have done better if receiving the President of the Federation. She had not expected such comfort – had not expected anything more than peace – and had entered the forest with only a pack on her back containing the bare necessities for a

76

travelling ethnologist, to which she had added a close-fitting robe of deep emerald and gold with a high neck and flowing sleeves in case there was a chance to wear it for Humphrey's delectation.

The chance was now. Breeches and boots were hardly ceremonious enough for the preparations in the court-yard which she observed from her window: a table of heavy, polished timber, seats of carved benches, magni-ficent silver. As night fell, four braziers set on poles gave clear red flames reflected in the table and the pool. Emerald and gold, she decided, were exactly right for the shapes and shadows beyond the flames. The High Commissioner's daughter swept gallantly out to join the family, somewhat embarrassed to find the Dowager still in her woollen sack of a garment though now wearing on her grey hair the same golden circlet as Humphrey with the badge of the perched owl, like a third barbaric eye, over her forehead.

The conversation ran easily over George's ambulance until Humphrey, sitting on her left, remarked:

'Not afraid of us any more, Thea?'

'No. To be here again is like coming home after – after all the agony of a hospital which tries to save and can't.'

'Do you care so much what happens to the immi-grants?'

'I care because we have failed so terribly. It was such a wonderful experiment to return them to the land of their dreams. I've grown up with it, you see. And now there's a people beaten and massacred and a girl going to be deported and imprisoned as a bit more example to them. And all it does is to turn them sullen. They won't work and won't speak to us and they don't care if they die of starvation so long as they do die.'

'We call that a General Strike,' Humphrey said.

Guelph added that he had joined the strike himself last time, that the Middlesexes couldn't always be allowed to have their own way.

'And bitterness doesn't remain?' she asked.

'Not long. It's an old tradition and it works. But we have never had to see what you have seen.'

She spoke more quietly, trying to lend herself to the calm of the forest.

'The dead were peaceful. It's not the sights – it's the lies. You watch the lies changing their faces like illness, even my father's face. How can they say he did this horrible thing?'

'Because he's a mystery to them, so powerful and yet so compassionate. What beats me is that they believe Pezulu Pasha did. He couldn't be anything but correct. A policeman doesn't rape. He nudges.'

Thea smiled, but the memories were too vivid. She shivered and broke down in a single deep sob.

'We shouldn't dine out of doors in September,' Humphrey said, 'but we go on as long as we can.'

He threw a rich cape of squirrel fur over her shoulders. She reached up a hand, ostensibly to adjust the collar, and imperceptibly held his.

'I am so weary of my world.'

'You could grow just as tired of this one, Thea.'

The Dowager had noticed the hand. George quickly explained that mamma never approved of anyone changing sides.

'Do have some more autumn raspberries, Thea,' Humphrey invited, also coming to the rescue.

'May I? And what is this wonderful stuff you eat with them?'

'Just something we eat.'

'Humphrey, you know I'm over all that.'

'Well then, it's cream.'

'No, it isn't. We eat cream too. My father had his specially made up for him.'

'But this is real cream. It comes out of cows.'

'How horrible!' Thea exclaimed, dropping her spoon.

'I knew you'd say that.'

He tried to take away her plate, but she stuck to it.

'No, Humphrey. I have to remember there is beauty in taste.'

'Miss Pretorius, you do *not* have to,' Guelph asserted. 'At this over-fruitful time of year I'd sometimes like to be a Euro-African and take a sandwich on the run.'

'But what my palate likes, Guelph, my mind doesn't. It's absurd that I should love the taste of your hare that's been hung for two months and not have the courage to look at it.'

'Two weeks, not months,' the Dowager corrected her. 'And in a cool place.'

'Well, whatever it is. And you are not to tell me what I am eating, Humphrey, until I have already raved about it.'

'So long as it isn't just bravado.'

The Dowager mentioned that in her experience bravado was the only reason why a sensible woman made a fool of herself.

Thea boldly met her eyes across the table.

'It may be why she begins.'

'Really, women are incredible,' Humphrey said. 'And all because I once brushed some maggots off a hare!'

Thea was about to turn on him, but realised just in time that he was well trained in pretending stupidity.

Occupied by the wisp of strain which blew across the table, they had not been listening to the forest. Guelph got up, his head bent to catch some distant sound. This time the message was clear.

'Black Rod! Black Ro-o-o-od! A stranger coming up the western path!'

'A stranger? We haven't issued any permits recently, have we, George?'

'It must be Pezulu's secret agent again, pretending to be an Inspector of Missions. Guelph, do you want to go to the mainland for a course in Higher Thought and take a sandwich on the run?'

'Not him, George. He won't be back ever.'

'Why not? He thought you'd seen the light.'

'That old bull in Brentford marshes had better be shot.'

'Oh no! He's rather a friend of mine and no worse than his herd. Those wild cattle only kill for fun.'

'I did tell the Inspector that he shouldn't camp by the river,' Humphrey confessed. 'But perhaps I wasn't convincing enough.'

A figure came staggering into the light of the braziers. His clothing was ripped by thorns and the tattered strips torn down by himself to tie the soles of his shoes to his bloodstained feet. The unshaven bristles on his face poked through a coating of mud. He stopped by

Humphrey, tried to stand upright but swayed with fatigue.

'Are you ... Middlesex?' he asked.

'I am. Are you aware, sir, that this is a radioactive prohibited area?'

'They say so.'

'You have come here alone and on foot?'

'I have.'

'Where from?'

'Avebury. I escaped.'

'Into the forest? You? A welfare unit? How did you find your way?'

'Compass.'

'How long did it take you?'

'Six days, I think. I may have lost count.'

'And it's me you have come to see? What's your name?'

'Alfred Brown.'

'And what's your crime? That unpardonable nationalism, I suppose.'

'His daughter shot at my father and he provided the arms,' Thea said coldly.

Alfred Brown had had only eyes for Middlesex. For the first time, he looked at the company, recognised Thea and hung on to the table to prevent himself collapsing.

'It isn't true,' he cried. 'Oh God, what was the use of coming here?'

'I am quite sure it isn't true, Mr Brown,' the Dowager declared. 'Can't see much of your face under all that slime, but you don't look to me like the kind of chap who'd give the job to your daughter. Do it yourself, you would! Humphrey, never mind the politics! He's our guest. Guelph, tell 'em to bring the joint back. George, he's bleeding all over the place. Clean him up!'

George replied that gin was better than cold water, grabbed the bottle and knelt at his patient's feet.

'All right, son!' he said as Brown's yell startled the forest. 'Dislocated toe that was. It won't give you any more trouble after a good night's rest.'

'I've no time. They've got me now.'

'Imagination, Mr Brown. Police are not allowed here without my permission,' Humphrey told him.

'I've heard things talking to me that probably weren't there, sir, but I'm warning you straight. I've got the Corrector on my tail.'

'Who the devil is he?'

'It. It's an it. They dropped it when they knew I must be in the forest. But it can't see very well what's under the trees.'

Guelph arrived with the remains of a sucking pig on its silver skewer and laid it before Brown with bread and wine.

'Thank you, madam. Thank you, sir. But it's time for talking that I want. I don't know if you're a father.'

'No, nor do I,' Humphrey replied.

As severely as was possible with his mouth full, Mr Brown explained that he was not referring to native customs whatever they might be.

'I'd like just to sit and eat. But I've come to you for help, whether it's your kind of manners or not.'

'Go ahead, Mr Brown! So it's as a father you think I could help, is it?'

'Aye, you see, Silvia is all what Mrs Brown has got

left. That's what broke me up when they put me inside. There's nothing I can do to make my people see sense, I said, so I'm free to think of myself and that meant Silvia and the missus. They don't expect you to try to escape, you know, because there's nowhere you can escape to. They'll never guess that one of us immigrants would tackle the bush alone, I thought, so I'll get a week's start on Pezulu Pasha. And here I am, and I ask you on my bended knees, sir, do something for my Silvia! You could rescue her and hide her here. She's a lovely girl, good as gold when it ain't politics.'

Thea assured him promptly that Pezulu would find her very quickly.

'Not if you said nothing, Miss Pretorius.'

'I cannot be irresponsible, Mr Brown.'

'I don't know what you think, Humphrey,' said the Dowager, 'but so far as I go I'd be glad to offer hospitality to any pure, young immigrant girl who is in trouble. She could have grandfather's old room.'

'Of course, mamma. But if Avebury could do nothing, what chance have I?'

'Protest! Work up your tribe and threaten!' Alfred Brown urged him.

'But they are my sons and daughters. Not in fact, but I'm responsible for them. And working them up, as you call it, seems to me a kind of murder of their souls.'

The whine of a little jet engine grew rapidly louder as some machine flew up the avenue. Alfred Brown stood up, dignified in spite of terror and his wounded foot.

'I told you. It's the Corrector. Thank you, Middlesex. We didn't see eye to eye, and never will, but thank you for your kindness. I . . . I'll try to behave decently.'

'Sit and eat Mr Brown! You're my guest. What's that thing doing, Thea, with all those dots and dashes and peeps?'

'Reporting its exact position, I think.'

'How does it know old Brown from me?'

'It's tuned to him. They'd have taken his personal wavelength at the same time as his fingerprints.'

The Corrector cleared the trees and began to circle Alfred Brown, starting up its numbingly monotonous chants:

'Stay where you are, Alfred . . . Stay where you are . . . It's no good, Alfred . . . it's no good.'

It looked detestably alive – short, black, about the size of an eagle, with compound insect eyes in front and quivering antennae on its back. The terrified Dowager threw a plate at it which astonishingly scored a direct hit and shattered.

'An intolerable intrusion,' she bawled. 'I shall speak to Pezulu about it.'

'Underground? Will that fix it?' George suggested. 'Stays? Stays over the spot? Well then, into the house and out again. Thing follows and gets caught between the doors.'

Alfred Brown whispered unsteadily as if the thing could hear:

'When it cannot get out it bores.'

'Laser, I suppose,' Humphrey said. 'Catching up fast with the Age of Destruction, aren't you? How close to the victim does it stay?'

'Close. Very close in front of his face wherever he turns.'

'What else does it do?'

'Nothing. It don't have to. You have the screaming jerks when it ...'

The Corrector homed in on him and remained motionless on station.

'Stay where you are, Alfred ... stay where you are ... it's no good, Alfred ... it's no good ... none of that, Alfred.'

'Too simple for city life. They'll never think of it. Brown, stand with your face a yard from the brazier flame! Guelph, get me the forge bellows!'

He handed Brown the silver cover of the great dish which had held the sucking pig.

'Use that for a shield and stand so that the Corrector is over the flame. And here's a fox-skin for your hand,' he added, ripping the cover off a chair, 'in case the handle gets too hot.'

Himself he crouched at the foot of the brazier and as soon as Guelph returned began to bellow with powerful puffs until the brazier glowed white. The Corrector hovered directly above and, evidently programmed to maintain its position, continued to hypnotise its prey.

'Stay where you are, Alfred ... it's no good, Alfred ... None of that, Alfred.'

One of its antennae, reaching out to register the accuracy of its distance, drooped. Something popped with a slight spark and a lens fell out of the compound eye.

'None of that, Alfred ... it's no good, Alfred ... good Alfred ... good Alfred ... good Alfred.'

'Nice, kind Alfred,' Humphrey mocked. 'But it's too late for apologies now, baby beetle! Does anybody know if it's likely to blow up?'

The Corrector began to scream. Under the circumstances the effect was harrowing, though the sound was familiar enough to any listener in Avebury trying to tune in to a remote station in the wilds of another Federation. Humphrey kept on bellowing. Thea and the Dowager shouted at him to get away from the thing. Guelph threw a coil of rope over its tail and walking backwards dragged it off and smashed it into the trunk of an oak.

Alfred Brown limped back to the table and tore in to more food.

'Got to have them things, all the same,' he said. 'You couldn't ask a policeman to go on searching this country day after day.'

'Why not? You did.'

'Because I had to. We aren't all like you, Mr Middlesex.'

'Well, you see, in order that my people may live I have to be sure who or what should die.'

'Aye. It's a shame we have nothing in common.'

'It does not matter at all that we have nothing in common when we're all in the same boat, Mr Brown,' the Dowager said.

'Does anybody know what mamma means?' George asked cheerfully.

'She means Britain,' Thea replied.

'Nonsense, girl! The immigrants know nothing about Britain. Guelph, give Mr Brown a hand to grandfather's room when he's finished.'

'I think we'd better put him away under a good thickness of earth,' Humphrey said.

The Dowager and Thea looked at one another with

sudden uneasiness. Alfred Brown, weary of his own body, was resigned.

'I can't argue about that. You have your own people to look after like you just said, and I thought it might happen. If you'd be kind enough to let Mrs Brown know, and then she won't keep worrying that I might be alive.'

Humphrey sat down by him and patted his shoulder.

'Alfred, I am shocked to find how much more sinister I seem to you than I really am. It's interesting too. I must give it some serious thought. George, shove Alfred on your stretcher and drive him at once to ... Guelph, what's old Giles' name for that bit of rough stuff where his cows will go to calve?'

'He calls it Golder's Green, but my aunt says it's Kilburn.'

'That's the place. And then get underground through the passage to the southeast.'

'We can't work our way through to West End any more,' George said. 'The spring tides fixed Leicester Square a couple of years ago.'

'Then just put the thickness of the Hampstead Hills between Alfred and the next Corrector. You needn't bother to go further.'

'It's a nasty place for him – those echoes, I mean.'

'He can take them in his stride. It's only the dead past that wants to see what you're up to.'

'Morning and evening are the worst.'

'What sort of echoes?' Thea asked. 'What do you imagine they say?'

'Nothing that I could ever make sense of. They flow like a mountain stream. Always in a hurry.'

The Dowager said goodnight, receiving a curtsy from Thea so graceful that it was hard to go on thinking of her as a flirtatious little scientist from the preposterous world of Federations. Guelph tactfully followed her, leaving Thea and Humphrey alone.

'You frightened us all,' she said.

'Surely not you?'

'For a moment, yes. Don't ever think you have nothing in common with the immigrants. You once told me you were the roots. Another tree could grow out of them. And then you spoke of moonlight on a stream that you would show me so that I could understand your other world.'

'Yes, the moon is full. I will show you as soon as my mother and my world know that you are in bed. Then come out quietly and we will go together to my church.'

She blew him a kiss and vanished into the house. What curious old-fashioned customs! There was no reason why host and guest should not walk together in the moonlight. Duty, perhaps. She had forgotten duty. She was the High Commissioner's daughter and, from the Dowager's point of view, a princess entrusted to her care by a prince. Charming! As if she was twelve years old. And probably the old girl wouldn't give a damn if Humphrey chose to be followed about by half a dozen little farmyard virgins as lovely as saplings and as dull.

And what about this church of his? An ancient tribe living by tradition might still go in for some solemnisation instead of the simple Federal formality of applying for a licence to bear children. Would she mind if it did? These people found the Federation comic in its unreality, while even brave and solid citizens like that Alfred Brown found the forest equally comic in its barbarism. On whose side was she? Did it matter? Her Humphrey must always have a foot in both.

Well, now that the house was quiet, what about the Dowager's princess climbing over the wall from school? Emerald and gold were all wrong for moonlight and running water. Some ingenuity was called for. She had chosen for that otherwise austere pack – why, Thea? – a long oriental nightdress of heavy white silk. With the silver squirrel cape which he had thrown over her shoulders and a wide silver belt, it was not too revealing. She looked in her mirror and let free her long hair. The moon in a black sky. Not bad. Ethnology permitted itself the ghost of a blush.

Standing unseen among his fellow trees, still and expectant as one of them, Humphrey watched her return to the courtyard. Divinely lovely she was. The word was no mere expression of exaggerated praise but sprang from the depths of his priestless religion. On her first visit he had deified Thea. She was a lunar goddess made visible to the believer: at night silver, in the day tawny as the low harvest moon. Such reverence for beauty was, he thought, like a tunnel of flowering branches which he had entered rarely, but often enough to recognise that the circle of sky at the far end grew larger and larger until the seeker was out to freedom. On this second visit he had learned that there could never be freedom. He had too much to give, like that stallion in George's story of the Age of Destruction which sired and died, the sole link between the past and a faint future.

He came out of the trees to meet her and bent to kiss her hand.

'Why so sad?' she asked.

It was no time for mystic visions of moon goddesses and stallions. He reminded himself promptly of the more mundane links between himself and Pretorius, himself and that brave and ridiculous Alfred Brown.

'Not sad. Solemn. I was worshipping.'

'Is the church you promised to show me here?'

'No, but there is a church for me wherever you are.'

He led her to the point where the avenue ended, seemingly at a blank wall of growth, and then along a path twisting through dwarf woodland so that its course a few yards ahead was always invisible. They came out onto a slope of short grass, beneath which was an oval pool mirroring the moon. A shallow stream entered and left it mysteriously under hanging branches of hazel, rippling into the depths of fine pebbles that showed as sparks of light.

'Sit down by me and you will feel my country.'

Thea did, oddly apprehensive. Yet it was a place which the casual wanderer, if he could ever have discovered it, would have passed with no more than a glance. There was nothing spectacular to be seen – no mountain peak, no waterfall, none of the commanding colours of the desert – only stillness. For the first time she understood the religion of these people: that in all beauty there was an element of fear – worship he called it – and in all fear an element of beauty.

'I can imagine a guardian spirit,' she said.

'Of course.'

'And do you bring her an offering?'

'Always. I offer myself. That is what beauty means.'

'And nothing over for a moon goddess?'

For hour after hour their enchanted bodies clung together until birds came down to drink, undisturbed, in the cold light of dawn. Humphrey murmured, 'Thea! Thea!', no words of endearment being as absolute as her name.

'Yes, my darling.'

'Were you awake?'

'I thought you weren't.'

'I have been wondering about ethnology ... well, scientists ...'

'What about them?'

'When I was a boy I used to poke woodlice with a pin to see how fast they could run.'

'How horrid of you!'

'So I sympathised. Your curiosity, I mean. I don't want you ever to feel ...'

'I think primitive man is just as stupid as civilised. And I am going back to the house.'

'What I am trying to say is ...'

'Let me go at once, Humphrey!'

'No, I won't ever. I love you. I love you so much that I don't want you to feel any duty to me. That's all I was trying to say. Come to me out of your world when you can and leave me when you must. I am here always, always for you.'

'Humphrey, stop it!'

'Why are you crying?'

'I don't know. Perhaps because you said all that before I could.'

The birds all rose and perched or looked for seeds

around the bank of grass at the pool's edge. They gave an impression of feathered naturalists who had been watching the long and complex mating of the human animal and had now decided that for this dawn it was all over. What had disturbed their observation was the powerful and impatient voice of the Dowager somewhere at the end of the blank avenue, threatening aggression.

'Humphrey! Humphrey! Where the devil is the boy?'

Only extreme urgency could have brought her out of bed before the sun. Telling Thea to take cover in case his mother started to battle through the bushes, Humphrey reached for his long leather jacket and vanished on a roundabout route to appear behind the Dowager as innocently as a dog with a bad conscience.

'And what are you up to?' she demanded. 'Nothing caught fire is there?'

'Just botany, mamma. I enjoy a little quick research before the day's work begins. Cross-fertilisation and that sort of thing. We have to contribute to science.'

'Do we? Damn it, only last year I sent the High Commissioner your grandfather's commode. And where are your trousers?'

'A precaution, mamma. The pollen sticks to them.'

'Well, couldn't you hear me yelling my head off? That Pezulu Pasha has just flown in. Landed at the bottom of the avenue. And what I've got to say to him he won't forget in a hurry.'

'Do you think he ought to know that his Corrector came down here?'

Humphrey had learned in early youth always to

ask his mother's advice before telling her what to do.

'Eh? What's that? You're very often right, Humphrey. Just like your grandfather! Of course he shouldn't know. What about that girl? She'll give the whole show away.'

'If I were you, I should let her go on sleeping till breakfast, mamma. She has quite enough of Tito Pezulu at home.'

'Ethnology! Pah! Any nice legends this morning, mum? And put your trousers on at once, Humphrey!'

She strode off to greet the Chief of Police. Humphrey, stuck with the choice of reaching the house unseen in a dash for trousers or wasting time in returning to the pool, was still wavering when Thea rose unexpectedly from a screen of impenetrable hollies alongside the avenue.

'Here they are,' she said. 'My Lord of Middlesex never noticed that he hadn't put them on, and I thought he might need them.'

'The Lord of Middlesex was busy with other matters, and is desolate to see that one lovely breast has been scratched in his service.'

'Could you manage to kiss it better while doing up that belt?' she suggested, and added after a short interval: 'I shouldn't give the whole thing away.'

'Of course you wouldn't. But Tito Pezulu charges in so blindly. Silence won't stop him, only emptiness. Like a bull which knows I am in the grass, but can't see me.'

'Will Brown be safe?'

'Yes. He and George make a good team. If one can't the other can.'

'He's the only immigrant I ever met who is as British as you.'

'My sweet, there's no resemblance at all between his Britain and mine.'

'How much is there between my father's Thea and yours?'

'We can't both love different human beings.'

'No. That's it.'

'But all old Brown thinks about are Laws of Nelson and self-government. Nothing essential and very dangerous. What does it matter who makes the kindly rules for welfare units and factories?'

'You're the only person who could make him see it. A woman dreams her lover-to-be,' Thea insisted vaguely, 'and when he really is her lover she knows at once whether her dreams are true.'

'I've seen men adored who had no more character than a pint pot full of lies and water.'

'But their women know it.'

'What are you trying to tell me, then?'

'That now I am sure. The you which quickens me and all your world would have the same effect on *my* world.'

The Dowager's voice, winging triumphantly through her own grey dawn, reached them before Pezulu's more obsequious responses. Thea vanished behind the screen of hollies.

Tito Pezulu was dressed for adventure in high boots and a dark green smock, its pockets stuffed with cartridges.

'How are you, Middlesex? Fun at night and up with the lark! It's never too early or too late for you. Alcohol and exercise – that's the life.'

It was not a reputation of which the Dowager approved.

'He is educating himself, Pasha, all the time. It's botany now – going around with a little paint brush interfering with laws of nature.'

Humphrey, however, assumed the male heartiness expected, which was invariably effective in avoiding the personal questions of curious academicians from the Federation.

'Too early for a drink, Pasha, do you think? Beer for breakfast?'

'I can't stop for breakfast, old boy. You'll have to forgive me. Just one little enquiry and I'm off.'

'Well, let's sit down on this tree trunk. Mamma, would you ask Guelph to bring us out a flask of your *old* sloe gin?'

The Dowager left them, giving to Pezulu the least ceremonious of the curtsies required by protocol.

'How's His Excellency's daughter?' Pezulu asked.

'Very devoted to her profession.'

'A pity for a little honey like that, isn't it? We could think of something better for her to do, eh?'

'For us it is so difficult to get over our racial prejudices. And His Excellency?'

'Tired. Very tired. If only he had trusted me to deal with all that scum, they would never have dared to raise their heads. But it's all over now. You're going to have this country to yourselves again.'

'We shall be very sorry to lose you and the High Commissioner.'

'Always courteous. Wonderful chaps you are. And what I like is that your faces are all so different. Now, it's bound to take time to ship all the welfare units back to Africa, and meanwhile we shall have to ask you not to entertain individuals.'

'I quite see that. Stands to reason.'

'Now do tell me – what happened to that Corrector?'

'I'm terribly sorry about him, Pasha. I told him not to camp in Brentford marshes. George is over there now, collecting the shreds.'

'Brentford marshes?'

'The Inspector of Missions.'

'My Corrector, I said.'

'Did I give him a permit?'

Pezulu explained in patronisingly simple language that it was automatic and could fly and hover. He omitted all details of how it worked, for he was not too sure himself.

'It was following the terrorist, Alfred Brown,' he went on. 'Its last reported position was very close to your house. It homed on Brown and my superintendent is certain he saw him on the screen just before the thermocouple melted.'

'It caught fire?'

'It can't catch fire. Bits of it melted.'

Melted. Humphrey's line of attack lay wide open. Tito Pezulu, though fearless on his own ground, was ready to half-believe any good story – invented as a rule by George and allowed to leak over the border – of improbable tigers descended from zoo escapes in the Age of Destruction, or of the blackest witchcraft.

'No flames,' Humphrey said thoughtfully. 'Heat transfers ... tele-something they call it ... Oh, not again! Those old virgins can't be at it again. Mamma assured me that they had given up sacrifice.'

'Sacrifice? I never knew ...'

'We don't talk about it. No, if I thought that was the explanation, I'd tell you. You're wasted in the police. Nobody understands us as you do.'

Pezulu accepted the compliment complacently, saying that years of experience counted, as he was always telling His Excellency who had the grave fault of seeing two sides to every question. One should give an order and have it obeyed.

'I never give any. I know what they want and they know what I want. And it works.'

'Look here, old boy. I don't want to press you about my Corrector.'

'Oh, that. But it's too absurd and wicked! Anyway, this Brown could not have survived. The wild cattle and the hungry lynx. And those pits going down into God knows what underground. Even I don't go there. And then in the Chiltern Hills there are whole colonies of our fierce native adder.'

Pezulu shivered involuntarily. Adders were unthinkable.

'But the Federation has nature reserves in Africa.'

'By God, we cleared all the snakes out of them! This nothingness full of everything is the most sinister place I have ever ...'

'That's why it isn't wise to frighten my people with things like Correctors.'

Pezulu glanced behind him. Nothing was there but the dark hollies fighting each other for space, and in front the first shadows of tall timber wriggling across the avenue.

'I – I love a long chat with you,' he said. 'But what are you getting at?'

'Myself, I'm very careful not to offend the Virgins of the Sun.'

'Who are they?'

'Perhaps they are called something else in the Federation. When the sun was seen again after the fog of the Age of Destruction, they claimed to have brought it back by sacrifice. And mother to daughter the tradition carries on.'

'What the hell have they got to do with my Corrector?'

'It's true that they'd be more interested in you. But of course you were all right so long as my mother was with you. That unaccountable heat made me think that ... but I don't see how. The only corpse they would work with died two days ago. Not fresh enough, you see.'

From the hollies came a faint, eerie, sobbing howl. Pezulu grabbed Humphrey's arm and stammered a question.

'Ssh! We must keep our heads,' Humphrey whispered. 'The sun will be up in a minute.'

He had a feeling that he had overdone it. That lynx-like wail – where on earth had Thea heard it? – was far too profane for the ancient mysteries of the Virgins of the Sun. He was saved from changing course by Guelph's footsteps navigating the undergrowth as lightly as if his pads were furred. Pezulu clung still more closely until Guelph appeared carrying a black bottle on a silver tray without any glasses. With a formal bow which suggested a long tradition behind it, he offered the bottle to the visitor who seized it and tipped a long draught down his throat. Pezulu opened his eyes wide and collapsed very gradually as his knees gave way.

'We ought to have warned him, Guelph. And before breakfast too! Well, it won't do him any harm.'

'The Dowager may have foreseen what would happen when she told me to present the bottle with no glasses. Shall I have him put in the sickroom?'

'Yes, Guelph, and see that he is surrounded by luxury and deference. Call him about midday with beer and a devilled partridge.'

Guelph bent his back and Humphrey lifted Pezulu, still smiling, into position.

With Guelph and his burden out of the way, Thea burst out of the hollies.

'That was very impulsive,' Humphrey said. 'He might have fired at the bogey.'

'I think it was disgraceful discussing me in that way,' she retorted.

'Oh, my racial prejudices!'

'Don't you dare laugh at me! It was not funny. A man of taste should be able to put Pezulu in his place without that.'

'On my way to the outer world?'

She was silent, but did not withdraw her hand when he kissed it. Then suddenly she asked him desperately:

'Humphrey, *would* you love me more if I were fair?'

He held the face of his moon goddess between his hands, saying softly:

'I cannot see what flowers are at my feet
Nor what soft incense hangs upon the boughs
But in embalmed darkness ...'

He stretched his hands apart so that her hair poured over his bent head.

' . . . guess each sweet
Wherewith the seasonable mouth endows
The grass, the thicket.'

'What strange, lovely old English! Is that from the anthology?' she asked.

'No. Just a torn page from what was once a book. But how did you discover the anthology?'

'The immigrants have it too.'

'Do they? That's one of so many things I did not know.'

Chapter VII

Humphrey stood at the edge of the forest, watching the tiresome neatness of Avebury and the white Residency on its little hill. He was too far away to notice in detail the emptiness of the streets and the closed gates of the factories, but even so there was a perception of stillness as if the town, that exotic and bustling imposition upon his Britain, was asleep. Thea had persuaded him to visit Avebury and to feel for some of those things he did not know – to poke it in fact as he had poked his woodlice to see how fast they could run – but it was no time for poking. He liked Pretorius and had occasionally made a courtesy call on the Residency, talking genially of nothing, asking nothing and going away. He had never interfered with the policy of the Federation or indeed showed much interest. Thea had told him that he would have the same effect on her world as on his own. He did not believe it.

No, it was not Thea but Alfred Brown who was responsible for his ride to the frontier, this damned Brown who had had the courage to throw himself upon the mercy of the forbidden forest. He had come as a guest to ask for help and patronage which could not be refused to any of his own native Britons. Why then should it be refused to a wretched welfare unit? No answer. So it was dishonourable to stand there hesitating, especially since Guelph had accompanied him and was looking for a lead. Anyway Brown was plainly innocent. A less likely terrorist could not be imagined.

On the open hillside facing his cover were two groups of immigrants, one lying down on the grass, either exhausted or at peace, another group further away, apparently arguing and gesticulating, among whom he recognised that intolerable crook, the Chancellor of the Exchequer in his arrogant purple uniform and frock coat. Nothing could exhibit more pretentiously the sham of their stupid nationalism.

The three spread out on the grass were near enough for him to hear something of what they were saying. Poor devils, they had been through the massacre on the terrace of the Residency and, at a guess, had stumbled out of hospital into the soft, healing air. One was grey and wasted, either from hunger or haemorrhage. Another stretched out a leg in plaster. The third had a bandage over the lower part of his face, and his speech, what little they could hear of it, was a muffled growl; he often raised himself on his elbows, looking enviously along the line of the forest and out between a pair of tall stones which framed the rolling down of Avebury.

'The wife and I used to picnic up here,' Hungry said.

They nodded approval. Leg remarked that he was thankful to be alive.

'Yes, me too. But it's queer that one can't die of sorrow.'

They thought that over in silence until Bandaged Jaw, remembering latent desires which daily life had frustrated, grumbled passionately and almost distinctly:

'I ought ... to have spent more time ... looking.'

'You don't know your luck till you have to leave it,' Leg said. 'There's a bit of hill above Benghazi which will always remind me of this.'

'The grass ... is ... different.'

It was the first time that Humphrey and Guelph had seen the results of armed rebellion. They were well used to accepting the normal run of accidents and death inseparable from their ancient freedom, but this resignation of the wounded seemed to call for pity and help.

'Good morning, chaps! Anything we can do for you?' Humphrey asked as they joined the group.

'Morning! Lovely day after the rain,' Leg answered.

'Very good for the roots.'

'Mine are dead.'

The other three, further along the hillside, walked over to inspect the new arrivals.

'Good Lord! It's a couple of natives!' Smith exclaimed.

Green said that there could be a story in it if they had time.

'Ah, Middlesex, you come upon us in a sad moment, a melancholy hour,' the Chancellor greeted him.

'I'm told it's the best time of year in the Mediterranean.'

'And in our hearts we shall carry Britain with us. My lambs, for the sake of your children, treasure these last days!'

'And leave it to you to tell 'em lies about why poor bloody Daddy has a wooden leg,' said Leg, turning away.

'I shall tell them that he gave his all. More he had not.'

'All. Not the half of it!' Smith declaimed. 'Is my spirit broken? Is yours? Never! The Federation is going to deport us. They are going to end what they call their generous experiment. Good! But before that we will have given them death in the darkness, death in their houses, death wherever a man walks alone.'

'And we have all the intellectuals with us,' Green added. 'All the noble force of liberalism on our side! Have you seen the moving protest from Federal authors?'

'Yes.'

'Well then!'

'I never noticed ... there was so much ... gold in the mist,' said Bandaged Jaw.

'You're all eyes these days,' Hungry remarked.

'Chum, I've time to use them. Talking ... hurts.'

'Are you staying on, Mr Middlesex?' Leg asked.

'We are staying on.'

'Could you tell me ... the name of ... those trees on the hill ... which are turn ... turn ... turning colour?' Bandaged Jaw mumbled.

'They are beeches.'

'Thank you. I like to know ... the name of what I love.'

'So do I.'

'It makes it easier ... to talk about them ... when I can talk again.'

'Well, look after 'em for us!' said Leg. 'I'm glad they aren't giving you any trouble.'

'Trouble? They've got those poor natives where they want them,' Smith declaimed to his audience. 'They could starve them out by carting away the manure heaps.'

'I never thought of that,' Humphrey replied. 'Given a road or a flying dung cart, I suppose they could. But they would never find their way back to Avebury.'

'You mean to say that you are with us?'

'You do like to divide things into two, sir.'

The Chancellor moaned piously:

'He who is not with us is against us.'

'So you are willing to help?'

Humphrey glanced at the three wounded, who had lost all interest in their former ringleaders.

'I have a lot in common with some of you,' he said.

The words slipped out more sharply than he intended and for the moment defied self-analysis. His opinion of the immigrants had only been one of disdainful toleration. He accepted the ideals of the Federation and the policy of the High Commissioner; Pretorius was right in his ruthless decision to expel the lot of them. And yet these poor devils with whom, as he had just said, he had so much in common, had also a right or dreamed they had a right – and were they not dreams which allowed a sufferer to live rather than exist? – to love the home which had once been theirs. They had become a race utterly different from his own people, but even so should be free as the birds and animals to lift up their hearts to the spirit of the land.

'We have failed. There's no point in denying it,' Smith admitted almost proudly. 'We were all wrong to engage the police and the army. What I want now is that hundreds of us should work in secret. Kill, kidnap, destroy – and then vanish! The Federation is too soft to stand that for long.'

Guelph warned that the British seemed to have mastered that technique before they were deported the last time.

'What is your authority for that?' Green asked.

'My aunt, sir.'

'Oh, legends! Quite!'

'We had better know who this fellow is before going any further,' Smith said.

'I am Black Rod, servant of the forest.'

'You still have servants down there?'

'We all serve. That must seem strange to you.'

'I'll say it does! You have to take in this world. Nobody is going to give you anything. But what do you do? Hold his hand when he's in trouble?'

'If required.'

'And he pays you for it in whatever you use for money?'

'He does. But I don't pay him anything for holding mine.'

'Guelph, I am amply repaid,' Humphrey protested.

'Observe, my lambs, the natives!' the Chancellor expounded. 'Is it not written in the Laws of Nelson that Manners Maketh Man?'

'Aye, and it's a shame the Assembly didn't remember that instead of screeching away like a bunch of tomcats,' Hungry said.

That set Smith off again. Waving his overworked arm, he told the eager trees that this was no time for manners when for the British every hour was an hour of suffering, every day a day of effort. Some time, victorious, they would have a use again for manners ...

The speech threatened to go on interminably, thus giving time for Humphrey to listen only to himself. This visit to Avebury, intended only to explore the intentions of the High Commissioner and, if the occasion offered, to plead for Brown's acquittal and any possible mercy for his Silvia, had now forced on him a wider objective. What could he do for these guests of Britain, these three who were saying farewell to a dead love?

Nothing. He was helpless. Or was he? If Thea had not insisted that he would be more effective without her, if she had been present and listening with her hand on his, she would never have let him be resigned to a lack of influence. She was too impressed, however, by the quality of leadership which she saw in him. Well, at least these immigrants were ready for it. They were leaderless, or soon would be.

'No doubt you are perfectly right,' he said to Smith, interrupting the flow.

'You understand me? You are educated?'

'My mother would tell you that I have been taught to lead and not to think. An all-round failure, I'm afraid.'

'You don't have to think. And we'll make it worth your while.'

'What do you want?'

'A hide-out in the forest. A headquarters which they will never suspect.'

'Will Alfred Brown join you in this campaign?'

'The martyr, Alfred Brown? Not he! He doesn't represent anything. Is he still alive?'

'Oh, yes. I've had some interesting talks with him. You wouldn't say he loved this country?'

'No. He thinks it's enough if he just gives himself.'

'I see. Now, Chancellor, you and I have known each other for some time. Off and on. I know what to do for you. But these two political leaders – are they responsible for this rising?'

'What man could do, they did, Middlesex.'

'Guelph, I think the Inspector of Missions' camp in Brentford marshes would be just right for these patriotic activities.'

'Very fitting indeed.'

'Always agree with him, don't you?' Green said. 'You ought to have more pride, a big chap like you.'

'I am not aware of lacking pride, sir. I am descended from Kings of England.'

'His aunt again!'

'My plans have changed, Guelph,' Humphrey told him. 'When these patriots are safely accommodated, pick up Alfred Brown at Golders Green and bring him here. He and I will go together to Avebury.'

'Town clothes?'

'They are in the saddle bags with the tent. I shall camp near here with horses till you come. Would you all three like to go with Guelph now?' he added to Smith.

'Let's take a look at it, Green. We shan't be missed. They don't even bother to search for us any more.'

'It's a long road, but very restful when you get there,' Guelph assured them.

Black Rod beckoned to the Chancellor, Smith and Green, and formally walking backwards his few official steps started the three on the march to the haunts of the wild cattle whose habits George had charitably excused by claiming that they killed only for fun.

Bandaged Jaw asked if he could accompany them just as far as the beeches.

'I'd go along with him,' said Hungry. 'The wife and I used to picnic down there.'

'Not yet, friend.'

'Have a heart and let us go! It's now or never.'

'Now or never – it's seldom that really turns up and one sees it.'

Leg winked at him, murmuring:

'Come off it! What about yourself?'

'Me? I just bumble along.'

'You bumbled a bit of all right with your hide-out. I wouldn't put it past you, terrorism. But not with that gang.'

'Not if you're a friend of Alfred Brown,' Hungry added.

Bumbling, Humphrey thought, was exactly what he

had been doing until he accepted that any interview with Pretorius must deal with far more than the fate of Brown and his daughter. Neither demand nor protest from an amusing forest barbarian would have any effect on that kindly but formidable man. A lightness of approach, an air of irresponsible unconcern should be his opening move, and then he should act out the image which Pezulu's fantasies had created: an image of geniality which disguised mystery and power.

Bandaged Jaw fixed his eyes on Leg, guessed at once what he suspected and tactfully changed the subject.

'Fine chap ... that Black ... Rod.'

'I'd like to see Mrs Brown's face when she hears her old man is in the bush.'

'Picked a harem for him, have you?

'Bow and arrow more like, and a nappy for his big bum!'

'Now if you and him was to get together, we'd all have a bit of fun,' Leg said to Humphrey.

'What sort of fun?'

'What we want, cock, the Federation can't give nor them three bastards either.'

'Put a name to it.'

'Ah, that's where you have me. I dunno.'

Though the reports of his Chief of Police were hard to believe, duty compelled Pretorius to take them – well, not seriously but with courtesy. The policy of resettlement had failed and he accused himself of too gentle a tolerance. That had led to the massacre at the Residency only halted by the fantastic behaviour of Aranda, out of keeping with the old-fashioned, half comic traditions of the military. There could be no more tolerance now.

He had decided to interrogate Silvia Brown himself for a second time. The first interrogation, immediately after the attempted assassination, had not been successful, but after weeks in the reformatory, kindly though the treatment was, defiance would have been tempered by boredom.

He was right in that. Her pink and white complexion had taken on a shade of grey and her blue eyes no longer sparkled. She slumped a little in her chair, whereas on her first appearance before him she had been tense as a young bitch in training and her chair a springboard for attack. This time, instead of the friendly gesture of sitting on the corner of his desk, he remained facing her on his official chair, emphasising authority. Tito Pezulu stood to her right and farther away was an Inspector taking notes of the interrogation. She was in the midst of a triangle of power.

After some personal questions on her political opinions, her education, and how and by whom she had been drawn into the criminal activity of nationalism, Pretorius handed over to Pezulu.

'Where are Smith and Green now?' he asked.

'I don't know. How should I?'

'What contacts had they with the natives?'

'None.'

'Did Smith and Green know Humphrey of Middlesex?'

'No.'

'But the Chancellor did?'

'That's a policeman's question. You put them for the

sake of putting them. You might as well ask me when the Chancellor learned to play the fiddle.'

Pretorius agreed with her. He sternly suppressed a smile and explained that Pezulu Pasha was suggesting that the Chancellor was the contact between her committee and the natives.

'But why? Those poor natives could not be any use to us.'

Silvia held the seat of her chair as if to keep herself from falling. Pretorius guessed rightly that it was exasperation rather than any faintness which affected her. He gave her his first smile and retired to the window with Pezulu.

'We must get it out of her before we let her see her father,' Pezulu said.

'I think she's telling the truth.'

'Believe me, sir – you can't trust to instinct in dealing with politicals. Play our last card!'

'It won't work.'

The two returned to their places. Pretorius, attracted by the youth and courage of his would-be assassin though disliking her British beauty, did his best to look fatherly.

'Now, I am not going to bargain with you, Miss Brown. Justice must take its course. If, however, you will tell me what you know of the relations between your secret committee and any native tribes under the leadership of Humphrey of Middlesex, I am prepared to recommend a reprieve to the President of the Federation.'

'I do not want a reprieve. There is nothing to live for.'

'Think of your mother! You may be all she has.'

'Have you killed my father?'

'You know very well that we do not commit murder,' Pretorius answered severely. 'Your father was in the care of the State for harbouring arms.'

'He was innocent. I told you. What have you done to him?'

'Nothing yet. He managed to escape to the forest,' Pezulu said with a shade of admiration.

'That's a lie! It's impossible to escape.'

Pretorius banged his desk.

'My good girl, he did!'

'What about your Corrector then? Oh, to think that I tried to shoot you! You're as futile as all your people.'

Pezulu ordered his Inspector to remove the prisoner until she calmed down. A remarkable temper she had, fortunately rare among the immigrants who treated the authorities with respect whatever they thought of them. The Inspector marched her off through a side door leading to the lobby of the private apartments.

Pretorius rose thankfully from his desk, saying that Silvia Brown knew nothing of any interest.

'I cannot understand what you've got hold of, Tito. I'm not even sure that your Smith and Green exist.'

'They exist all right. And if I could lay my hands on those two they'd have a nasty accident while trying to escape.'

'Yet you're afraid to arrest Alfred Brown!'

'I'm watching his contacts.'

'I've been told that by some security man or other once a week for two years.'

Pezulu pointed to papers in the High Commissioner's

pending file and ventured to say that he would find security reports still of value if he were to read them.

'Same old stuff! A reliable source reports that ... Confirmation has been received that ... A frequents B, B frequents C, therefore A knows C.'

'Look here, sir – it's simple. Middlesex is seen strolling openly with Alfred Brown outside Brown's house. The pair of them are run in. Middlesex makes himself comfortable and sends for me. I turn him loose with apologies. He refuses to be separated from Brown. So I give Brown a temporary pass.'

'But why?'

'Because we cannot afford to offend Middlesex.'

'Offend him? Naturally I do not want to offend him. But what beats me is that the mere presence of this beer-swilling barbarian in the capital seems to paralyse the lot of you.'

'Where's the Chancellor? We don't know. How did Middlesex get hold of Brown and short-circuit my Corrector? We don't know. And whatever you like to say about reliable sources, it's a fact that Smith and Green are with him.'

'Well, I am not standing any nonsense from Middlesex. And I have kept him waiting long enough to make that quite clear, I hope.'

He pressed the button to summon Julian Cola, his ADC, who took a little longer to arrive than usual and left the double door slightly open behind him as if to hear any disturbance in the anteroom.

'Julian, send in Humphrey of Middlesex and the man Brown.'

'Yes, sir. I am afraid they are no longer here. It may take a minute or two.'

Pretorius had a sudden vision of the barbarian prince and the father of his assassin contemptuously wandering round the Residency to examine the guard posts.

'You will see that it takes less, Julian. I am prepared to receive them *now*. What the devil are they up to?'

'Middlesex insisted on using the time to teach the staff an old British game.'

'A game? In the anteroom?'

'Down the corridor, sir. He calls it French cricket.'

'*French* cricket? Oh, one of their ceremonies before business, no doubt.'

'Miss Theodosia would know, sir. But you make a tight ball of paper and tape. You then obtain a stick, ruler or other narrow implement. The first player tries to hit with the ball the legs of the second player, who defends them with the implement ...'

From outside the majestic double door came the patter of quick footsteps and the thud of a heavy man hitting the floor.

'Well caught, Alfred!' exclaimed Humphrey's echoing voice. 'What a dive! Cola, you're in.'

The ADC slid out before the High Commissioner's words could reach him.

Chapter VIII

Pretorius, still simmering with suppressed indignation, was annoyed by the elegance of Humphrey of Middlesex, whose tunic was cut to a perfection which Pretorius himself had never achieved and plain white in colour. That was an added impertinence. The High Commissioner looked with more sympathy at Alfred Brown, of whom one could only say that he was a normal citizen of Avebury wearing the usual monotonous clothing in which crude colours were the only sign of an individuality.

He extended a hand which Humphrey shook with a ceremonious bow and a charming smile, saying that he hoped they had not made too much noise. Pretorius was compelled to reply that he regretted having been compelled to keep them waiting. He did not offer a hand to Alfred Brown, but merely indicated a chair.

Humphrey turned to Pezulu Pasha, remarking how nice it was to see him again so soon.

'I've not had a look at you in our clothes before,' Pezulu replied. 'They suit you.'

'Thank you. You see, I might be spending a little time in Avebury and I hate seeming different to everybody else.'

Pretorius, not to be outdone in courtesies, commended Mr Brown for voluntarily returning to custody.

'I tell you what . . .' Alfred began.

'Alfred, it's a very small point, but . . . His Excellency,' Humphrey corrected him.

'I tell Your Excellency what. Before I met the natives I didn't know what I wanted. Now I do know.'

'What you wanted? I don't understand.'

'I'm all set for home.'

'So you see that, at last. Factory, home, recreational activity – all much the same wherever you are. What you call patriotism is objectless.'

'Aye. You don't need to be always kissing your girl in public.'

Pretorius was thankful for a chance to be generous. It was absurd to stand on his dignity, always unwelcome, because of this French cricket.

'Very well, Mr Brown, if that's how you feel, the unproven case against you can be dropped and you may return to the mainland whenever you wish. Let's see – where was it you came from?'

'Tunis Garden City.'

'Very well managed, I believe.'

'Smooth as bloody grease! But me, I'm staying here.'

'That is out of the question.'

'No, Excellency,' Humphrey interrupted quietly. 'To a man as broad-minded as your daughter insists that you are, nothing is ever out of the question.'

'Middlesex, I'm afraid you do not realise that you are consorting with criminals.'

'You have to mix with politicians too. It doesn't affect either of us, I hope.'

Pretorius gave his first genuine smile and asked what exactly he had been up to.

'Just listening to some of these welfare units. By the way, Pezulu Pasha, don't blow the heads of those two just when they were expecting promotion for grabbing Alfred. They were quite right to arrest me too. Hadn't the faintest notion who I was. Ought to have been dressed in goatskins or something.'

'And this canvassing of yours – what is its object?' Pretorius asked.

'To suggest to these immigrants that there's a lot in Your Excellency's point of view. It doesn't make a pig's tail of difference to them whether they are governed by the Federation or a self-conscious little Assembly of their own. Their food comes from factories, their thought and art and music from factories. And if you could colour their eyes blue you'd be making them in factories.'

'That's off the point, Middlesex. You are attacking our common civilisation.'

'I am. It has given my people nothing they really want, and is now going to deprive them of what they do.'

'*Your* people?'

'Yes. With all these politics in the way, I couldn't see that they loved the place.'

'Oh, not that again!' Pretorius sighed.

'Take Alfred Brown's daughter, for example! I haven't met the girl. Hysterical, I should think. But I'm told that when she landed she kissed the ground. Absurdly emotional of course, but from the heart. Shooting at you wasn't.'

'In any case I cannot understand this obsession with geography.'

'I can't either when you put it like that. Ask your daughter!'

'She's all right, of course, in your absence?'

'Oh, yes. Smith and Green won't do her any harm.'

Pezulu had reported their presence in the forest as a fact to the High Commissioner, but in reality it was no more than a rumour which he wanted Pretorius to take seriously and consider Humphrey of Middlesex as a potential ally. He was appalled to find the rumour true.

Pretorius himself was silent for a moment. His confidence that the revolt of the immigrants had been crushed for all time was in shreds. If there was any confidence about, it was Humphrey's which must be immediately shattered. The only possible response to it was power. He allowed full play to his earlier resentment.

'You will surrender those two instantly.'

Pezulu stood up and made the gesture of advancing on Humphrey with a couple of steps.

'Together with the Chancellor!' he demanded.

'Don't tell me you want *him* back!'

The Chief of Police stared into that impenetrable face with its air of courtesy and amusement and resumed his seat.

'The return of Smith and Green is a *sine qua non*,' Pretorius insisted.

'A what, your Excellency?'

'An essential.'

'Latin?'

'I really do not know.'

'Sounds like it. We still learned Latin in the tribal college.'

Pretorius, sidetracked by his enlightened interest in all that concerned the history of the natives since the Age of Destruction, controlled his impatience and asked if Humphrey understood it.

'No, I can't say I do. It's supposed to discipline the mind.'

'What you all need is sound technical instruction to Certificate level.'

'But one can pick that up any time.'

'Quite, quite, but –' Pretorius pulled himself together; 'Middlesex, after two years of casual dealings with you I am accustomed to approach business through a number of pleasant irrelevancies. And when I have the time I enjoy it. But if you have come here with some unwise proposal or ultimatum, get on with it!'

'Oh, that! Ultimatum sounds like Latin too. Well, what I did come to say was that I could offer you peace or civil resistance based on London.'

'There is no London.'

'That is why it will be so very expensive to suppress us.'

Pretorius realised that his best available weapon was charm against charm. He was aware, he said, that Middlesex and his tribe had been unsettled by all the excitement in Avebury. He did not want to appear patronising for he knew well that there were aspects of their culture of value to the future. But they were only two generations removed from bar . . . – well, the free life of natural man, and he did ask them to think whether they might not be out of their depth.

'Hopelessly, Your Excellency, hopelessly! I hate making anybody do what he doesn't want to. But here are my *sine qua nonni*, or *nonna* perhaps. Deportation to be stopped. Young Silvia to be released. Alfred Brown and myself to be Special Commissioners advising you on the permanent settlement of the immigrants.'

'And dismissal of Pezulu Pasha,' Alfred added.

Humphrey calmed down Pretorius with a genial gesture, implying that they must both be patient with old Brown, and turned amicably to the Chief of Police.

'I do hope I shan't offend you, Pezulu Pasha, if I say that I usually know what you will do and can make a good guess at what you will say.'

'If you mean that I am on the side of law and order, I am. And proud of it!'

'Loyal, energetic and quite incorruptible, Alfred. And that's about all anyone can ask.'

'Well, if you say so. Provided it ain't me who has to deal with him. All right, power to dismiss will do.'

'We will now cut this short,' Pretorius said. 'I have no authority to grant any of this nonsense.'

'The Federation is in such a flutter that it will accept whatever Your Excellency recommends.'

'I do not recommend impractical folly.'

Pretorius had always wondered how Middlesex preserved his power, for he knew only the smile which accompanied social ease. He had not previously met the smile which accompanied action. The subtle change in his opponent's face reminded him of a cat with the claws unsheathed whose power to strike was plain and intentions incalculable; playful they could be, or deadly.

'Then I offer you Smith's policy which is severely practical,' Humphrey replied.

'And that is?'

'Resistance to the death based on my territory! Black Rod whom I have attached to the Chancellor calls it terrorism. You can always take one of them with you. That's a fragment of St Winston though your daughter says he was only a symbol of virility. We shall give you death in your houses, death in the darkness, death wherever a man walks alone. We shall destroy your industry and communications and then – vanish!'

In spite of his alarm Pretorius responded bravely:

'Middlesex, by this time I can – unfortunately – recognise the sound of hatred in a voice. It is not in yours.'

'But I do not hate you. I like and admire you. And when I string you up from a tree in the course of my duty I shall not be able to trust my voice. Green will have to speak for me.'

Pretorius looked at Tito Pezulu for help but the appeal went unanswered. The Chief of Police never interfered in matters of high policy – a strategy which had served him well in the past, and at times had allowed him to come to the rescue.

'Middlesex, you have not been in the capital for the last month. I think a talk with General Aranda might bring you back to sanity.' Pressing a button of the desk transmitter he added: 'Aranda, can you come up a minute?'

'I will not stay in the same room as that butcher!' Brown shouted.

'Butcher? Only his duty, Alfred. But not one of us in this room would have dreamed of marching out alone to meet that fearless woman. Gallantry answered to gallantry. It was called chivalry once. I've read of it but never quite knew what the word meant.'

'You didn't? Who bellowed the flames until his hair was singed?'

'That was hospitality to a stranger. But for a soldier like Aranda chivalry is an instinct. Funny how a trade can die, and yet its finest tradition carries on.'

Brown, unaffected by such niceties, repeated that he would not stay in the same room. For the first time Pretorius lost his temper. He had no patience with a man so unforgiving that he did not even try to understand.

'Then you can leave it, damn you!'

Alfred Brown stamped straight to the small door which led to the private lobby and flung it open.

'Not that way!' Pezulu barked too late.

Seeing his daughter and the Inspector of Police,

Brown turned with blazing eyes and clenched fist.

'Now that's the end of it, ye pair of crooks!'

Humphrey stood back and looked through the open door.

'If only you had told me what was delaying you both, my dear Pezulu,' he said. 'It's so embarrassing. The very least you can do now is to invite the girl in. It's no good pretending she doesn't exist.'

For the moment, Pretorius and Pezulu were dominated by his casual acceptance of the incident as a mere social blunder. Neither protested when he called to the Inspector and prisoner to come in. Silvia's face lit up when she saw her father, but she controlled her reaction as Britannia should and stood defiantly in the doorway.

'Come in!' Humphrey repeated smiling. 'There's no catch about it.'

Britannia was still suspicious, but defiance looked painfully like sulks.

'Be your natural self, girl! I can't run this show if you aren't.'

At last she ran to her father and clung to him in tears. Pretorius, feeling more and more keenly the desecration of his seat of government, exclaimed that this was intolerable. And then the slippery Middlesex, impossible to pin down, deliberately chose to misunderstand him.

'Yes, I haven't a daughter myself,' Humphrey said. 'But I do understand how you must feel. Take her back to the other room, Alfred, and don't bother if the Inspector writes down every word you say. It won't make any sense, you know.'

When they had gone the High Commissioner tried to

keep in mind that only ten minutes ago he had decided that his best weapon was charm against charm.

'I hope, Middlesex, that at home, too, your influence ...'

'You have talked to my mother?'

'I have once had the honour of listening to her.'

General Aranda entered by the private lobby. His excellent military manners prevented him from commenting on the curious sight of a pretty child crying in the arms of an apparently prosperous citizen of Avebury, of the type to make a reliable sergeant, while an Inspector of Police looked abstractedly out of the window. Pretorius, seeing that no questions were to be asked (did Aranda think she had been beaten up or recruited unwillingly for the High Commissioner's bed?) made no reference to the encounter.

'Oh, Aranda,' he said, 'I believe you have not met Humphrey of Middlesex.'

They greeted each other most cordially, Aranda remarking that he had heard a lot about Humphrey from Pezulu Pasha.

'He should have brought you to see me.'

'Ha ha, yes! I'd have liked to study that little problem on the ground.'

Pretorius asked what problem.

'The Corrector I told you about,' Pezulu answered. 'I put it up to military intelligence.'

Humphrey's enigmatic smile was really one of private enjoyment; if the authorities chose to consider it ruthless, so much the better.

'I wish you'd come over to the mainland with me and talk to the backroom boys,' Aranda said.

'Let's give them a taste of the wilderness, General! It would make such a change for them.'

Pretorius broke in impatiently:

'Aranda, I must warn you that the native British put a high value on these little polite exchanges. They mean nothing. I wanted you here because Middlesex has just threatened to hang me.'

'Good Lord! Where?'

'On a tree.'

'He is under arrest?'

'No, no, no! He hasn't published it,' Pezulu protested hastily.

'Published what?' Humphrey asked.

'Your threat to hang the High Commissioner. If you published it you'd be run in under Paragraph 16A.'

'Oh, that's all right. We never publish anything till we've done it.'

'I wish I had you on my staff, sir,' said Aranda.

'Gentlemen, these irrelevancies ...' Pretorius began.

'I am so sorry, Excellency. Now, you wanted the General to explain something to me.'

'Middlesex has presented me with a childish ultimatum, Aranda. If I do not recommend his terms for acceptance by the Federation – which I have no intention of doing – he means to support a band of assassins in his territory to creep out of the trees by night and kill and destroy ...'

'And he's got the leaders of the immigrants there already,' Pezulu added.

'I want you to tell him in your precise military way, just as you would tell me,' Pretorius continued, 'how many hours it would take to annihilate the lot of them.'

'Normal civil revolt? Days, not hours, sir. Isolate the area. Destroy all food factories from the air. Wait for surrender. And that's all.'

'They have no food factories,' Pretorius snapped.

'In any case their supply problem ...'

'To hell with their supply problem! Exterminate them!'

'Only a matter of logistics, sir. Train the men, cordon off half the island and stop the boltholes! Then drive your roads through the forests. I could defoliate them if it wasn't against international law.'

'Burn the trees to the ground!'

'Can't, sir. Never enough summer. But all quite feasible provided the Federation will pay for it. Extermination would not take more than four or five years assuming always that they have no defence against the searching type of Corrector.'

'Only our simple little devices,' Humphrey admitted modestly.

'The backroom boys think they've got it now.'

'Yes, the principle is so obvious. If electronics can affect the human brain, then it stands to reason the human brain can affect electronics.'

'Aranda, we can discuss telepathy whenever you like,' Pretorius interrupted impatiently. 'But all the heavy industry of the native British is the hammer and the forge.'

'And that comes near magic, too, if you ask me,' said Pezulu.

'My dear Tito!'

'It's all very well, sir, but I like facts, and down among the trees there never are any. They don't reason or eat or behave as we do and I don't know how much to believe. Nor would my police. They'd panic or they'd fraternise. The trouble with Middlesex is that he carries the darkness about with him and pretends it's light. I'm ready to exterminate him here and now, and if I can't trust my voice you can do the apologising. But what alternative does he offer?'

'You suggest I surrender? To a barbarian beyond the pale of civilisation?'

Humphrey at once broke in with every appearance of being shocked:

'Excellency, I never dreamed of such a thing. Are we British immigrants? Surrenders, insults, protests, Laws of Nelson – must we talk like that just because I call on you informally with a very tentative proposal?'

The High Commissioner gasped with despair. The other two opened their mouths, searched for anything more than a clearing of the throat and were unable to find it. The sudden silence must have been noticed in the anteroom where Julian Cola had apparently been holding off interruption by a visitor who now considered that there was a gap in the discussion which she could reasonably fill. One half of the double door was largely obstructed by a back view of the Dowager of Middlesex, who was still addressing Cola.

'Nonsense, young man! You look after the boss's daughter for another minute or two. Got to prepare him, haven't I? You can't take these things as calmly as we do. He'd have a fit if she came barging in here before I had time to warn him.'

The Dowager closed the door firmly, turned and swept her most impressive curtsy to Pretorius.

'How are you, Excellency? I've brought your daughter back. It's all very well, Humphrey, for you to tell me not to let her out of my sight, but I never could do anything with George when you aren't there. Sticks the girl across a pony!'

'Across what?' Pretorius demanded.

'A pony. And then she goes and cuts an arser and breaks her arm! George set it without trouble. He's as good as any of your doctors so long as it's before dinner. But I knew how you would feel. If she were my daughter and she'd fallen down a community slide or whatever you've got to fall down – damned little if you ask me with all the care you take of yourselves – I'd want her back home at once.'

'You left my daughter at the mercy of a wild animal?'

'Fourteen-year-old gelding, and a green road. But you know what they are like. Surface liable to fall in. May be only a rabbit hole to start with and after a bit of rain you find yourself looking down a fifty-foot drop with a whole lot of bones and rotten metal at the bottom.'

'Your people's disregard for human life is atrocious!' Pretorius exclaimed, and would have developed his revulsion to the would-be insurgent's mother if Julian Cola had not held the door open for Thea.

Her left arm was in a sling with the ends of two splints sticking out from a bandage grubby with the reddish stains of dead leaves and blackberries caught up by swift passage through the forest. She looked a little pale but none the less alluring for that, since in her hair a crescent of ivy had twined itself, fit to crown a nymph of the green roads.

Pretorius rushed to her, pitiably demanding whether they had any proper antibiotics.

'Oh, some mushrooms which Guelph's aunt brewed in a saucepan. Humphrey, it's nothing at all.'

'My darling, George must have hurt you horribly.'

'No, he stuffed me full of gin first. It only hurt afterwards when I was sick.'

Pezulu and Aranda exchanged sly and joyous glances.

'Middlesex, this is beyond...' Pretorius began pathetically.

'Don't worry, Excellency! George would never have let her go if she wasn't fit to travel. The affection of the guest for the host,' Humphrey added vaguely, 'and the host for the guest – customary, you know, but sometimes we express it strongly. I cannot tell you how sorry I am. I thought of the Chancellor, but ponies never entered my head.'

Meanwhile Thea had coolly summed up a disquiet in the room which had nothing to do with herself.

'Without a hostess, father, you are quite lost,' she said.

Followed anxiously by Humphrey, who seemed to be jealous of the sling and ready to carry the broken arm himself, she slid back a panel to reveal racks of glasses together with flasks in the bright colours of flowers. Pezulu and Aranda made thankfully for the bar. Pretorius and the Dowager were left behind, discreetly inspecting each other.

'Madam, you have been most kind,' said the High Commissioner respectfully.

'You don't like the colour of *my* face, do you?'

'I beg your pardon.'

'I said: you don't like the colour of my face.'

'I find it – er – most exotically – er – fascinating.'

'And I don't like the colour of yours. That girl and Humphrey, eh? Wouldn't suit either of us, eh?

'You thought the affection was a little more than customary?'

'Stuck out a mile! Can't be anything serious in it, though. Always doing the rounds with me she was, except when she had gone off to bed. What's the boy come to see you about?'

Pretorius hesitated, uncertain of how much she knew.

'He was, shall I say, emphasising your native disregard for human life. And among other things he wants me to release Silvia Brown.'

'Just like his grandfather! First one knew of what he wanted was when he'd got it. Pretty, is she?'

'To British taste irresistible, I should say.'

'With a sound, solid father like hers there can't be much wrong. She shouldn't have taken a pot at you of course, but a day or two after rabbits will soon get all that out of her system.'

'If she were in your charge, do you think you could . . . ?'

'Of course I could! Clean young British girl like her – she can run the Little Sisters for me. They swear an oath to keep the paths open and the maps up to date. Keeps 'em out of mischief!'

'That does not involve permanent celibacy?'

'Lord, no! Humphrey used to take a great interest in the Little Sisters.'

Thea, chatting gaily to Aranda, had kept one ear

open to what her father and the Dowager were saying. She firmly interrupted:

'What would you like to drink, Dowager?'

'Gets the title right every time, Excellency. Too formal but she does try. All made of flowers are they, Thea? Queer thing, civilisation! Nothing between daisy water and jet alcohol! Make mine half-and-half. Half-and-half for the Dowager of Middlesex!'

Chuckling with laughter and arm in arm with an embarrassed Pretorius, she dragged him to the bar. There was nothing for it but to show himself decisive, and the only chance for peremptory action was Little Sister Silvia Brown.

'Middlesex, I am glad there has been a moment for tempers to cool,' he said. 'I have decided to release Silvia Brown unconditionally – a sort of thank-offering for my own daughter's escape, shall we say?'

'Very generous indeed of Your Excellency! Only a really strong man could have done that!' He strode to the private door and threw it open. 'Come on in, both of you! Alfred, your patience and self-control have persuaded the High Commissioner to pardon Silvia.'

Alfred and Silvia entered the seat of authority, followed by the Inspector who looked at his chief for orders.

'Just remain outside,' Pezulu murmured. 'There could be circumstances in which I shall need you.'

Humphrey ironically raised his glass to Pezulu, appreciating the threat.

'Excellency, I never thought you had it in you!' Alfred Brown exclaimed.

'And you remember this, young Silvia,' Humphrey

added. 'As soon as we stopped threatening him, Ali Pretorius was able to be his natural, kindly self.'

'I will not accept my pardon unless my people have it too!' she yelled.

'But you can't force 'em to lock you up and monkey with your brain box, girl. What you need,' the Dowager prescribed, 'is a month with us to see how the humble half of the British live.'

Thea protested that it was late for her to start tribal life.

'What have *you* got to do with it?' Silvia asked.

'I was only trying to help you.'

'So you think I'm in need of care and protection!'

'Of course not! You're an experienced revolutionary.'

'She's eighteen,' her father said bluntly.

'And it would be a pity if she came under the influence of Smith and Green again,' Humphrey added.

The Dowager asked who the devil were Smith and Green.

'Some immigrants whom Black Rod is looking after, mamma.'

The High Commissioner heated up again.

'Before I even listen to what you may have to say Smith and Green will be handed over to me.'

'Alive or dead,' Pezulu insinuated.

'Couldn't this be treated as a routine police matter?' Humphrey suggested. 'Well, give-and-take between the Pasha and myself?'

Pretorius refused. Silvia stormed that it was unthinkable, that Humphrey of Middlesex was not to hand them over.

'Now, now, girlie,' said Alfred Brown, 'I give you my word that he won't.'

The High Commissioner delivered his final judgement.

'You, Brown, and your wife and daughter will go back to Tunis Garden City, and you, Middlesex, to your settlement.'

'My father!' Thea protested.

'You must understand how serious this is, Thea. Middlesex threatened to hang me.'

'Excellency, it was *not* a threat. I said that if I was compelled to do so I should be unable to trust my voice.'

'And what had you threatened him with?' Thea asked Pretorius.

'Extermination!' Humphrey answered as if shocked by such brutality.

'My father – no!' she protested.

What game her Humphrey was playing she could not guess, but strongly suspected that the High Commissioner was the woodlouse being tickled to see how fast it could run. Both must be brought to order.

'Oh, but this is beyond belief!' she cried, pretending horror.

'Middlesex, drop this lunacy!' Pretorius appealed. 'These units are so used to welfare. They are not trained to create anything for themselves. They couldn't understand your way of thinking.'

'They are passionately fond of their little gardens.'

'By God, they are!' Aranda agreed. 'A chap put in some marvellous roses round the mess.'

'Always these irrelevancies!' Pretorius complained. 'You can't settle them in the forest. They are terrified by it. Will somebody talk sense? You, Mr Brown, you at least are an able politician. Just what *is* your proposal? What powers do you want for the Special Commissioners you mentioned?'

'Advisory.'

'And if we don't take your advice?'

'You take the consequences,' Humphrey said.

'Then you need us still?'

'My personal relations with the High Commissioner should be as close as between a father and a son.'

Pretorius looked suspiciously from Thea to Humphrey, but their bland smiles could not be interpreted. He took refuge in economics.

'But you are asking – if I understand you at all – for political responsibility without financial. That will get you nowhere.'

'Is there such a thing as social responsibility?'

Thea replied that once there was, and it was called monarchy.

'Absolute power?' Pretorius asked.

'In Britain, we think, the monarch had no power at all. His duty was to keep a sense of shame in those who had.'

Alfred Brown chuckled.

'You could do that, lad,' he said. 'Just keep it growing but don't call it anything. Slowly does it. That's what I have always told them.'

'But what is to grow?'

'The nameless,' Humphrey replied. 'The nameless, as Alfred says. What once flowered and could again.'

'And if I offer you Britain as it was – to grow in your own way without Avebury or immigrants?'

135

'No. I will not have the immigrants cleared out.'

'But you hate their childish, dangerous patriotism as much as I do. You don't care whether they have self-government or not.'

'Patriotism? Government? What do they matter to us, the last few British?' Humphrey answered slowly. 'Let us be free to love and we want no other freedom. Do you make war for the sake of the long shadows of elms upon the evening grass? Yes, we would. Will you die for the sake of the bare western downs folded around the sheep? Yes, I will. Don't ask me the logic of it – there is none. Do you believe that in the days of their greatness the British ever cared for trade, for towns, for power? That was as a man buys jewels for his wife. Only the wife remains now, and she was all they ever wanted. Perhaps they, too, became towards the end like these unhappy freedom fighters, losing every day a little of the power to love. That union with their land, for me never broken, is the right of my people. No law, neither yours nor theirs, can give it to them. If Alfred is right it may be, may be that I can.'

FOR THE BEST IN PAPERBACKS, LOOK FOR THE

In every corner of the world, on every subject under the sun, Penguin represents quality and variety – the very best in publishing today.

For complete information about books available from Penguin – including Pelicans, Puffins, Peregrines and Penguin Classics – and how to order them, write to us at the appropriate address below. Please note that for copyright reasons the selection of books varies from country to country.

In the United Kingdom: For a complete list of books available from Penguin in the U.K., please write to *Dept E.P. Penguin Books Ltd, Harmondsworth, Middlesex, UB7 0DA*

In the United States: For a complete list of books available from Penguin in the U.S., please write to *Dept BA, Penguin, 299 Murray Hill Parkway, East Rutherford, New Jersey 07073*

In Canada: For a complete list of books available from Penguin in Canada, please write to *Penguin Books Canada Ltd, 2801 John Street, Markham, Ontario L3R 1B4*

In Australia: For a complete list of books available from Penguin in Australia, please write to the *Marketing Department, Penguin Books Australia Ltd, P.O. Box 257, Ringwood, Victoria 3134*

In New Zealand: For a complete list of books available from Penguin in New Zealand, please write to the *Marketing Department, Penguin Books (NZ) Ltd, Private Bag, Takapuna, Auckland 9*

In India: For a complete list of books available from Penguin in India, please write to *Penguin Overseas Ltd, 706 Eros Apartments, 56 Nehru Place, New Delhi, 110019*

In Holland: For a complete list of books available from Penguin in Holland, please write to *Penguin Books Nederland B.V. Postbus 195, NL – 1380 AD WEESP Netherlands*

In Germany: For a complete list of books available from Penguin in Germany, please write to *Penguin Books Ltd, Friedrichstrasse, 10 – 12, D 6000, Frankfurt a m, Main 1, Federal Republic of Germany*

In Spain: For a complete list of books available from Penguin in Spain, please write to *Longman Penguin España, Calle San Nicolas 15, E – 28013 Madrid, Spain*

A CHOICE OF PENGUIN FICTION

Monsignor Quixote   Graham Greene

Now filmed for television, Graham Greene's novel, like Cervantes' seventeenth-century classic, is a brilliant fable for its times. 'A deliciously funny novel' – *The Times*

The Dearest and the Best   Leslie Thomas

In the spring of 1940 the spectre of war turned into grim reality – and for all the inhabitants of the historic villages of the New Forest it was the beginning of the most bizarre, funny and tragic episode of their lives. 'Excellent' – *Sunday Times*

Earthly Powers   Anthony Burgess

Anthony Burgess's magnificent masterpiece, an enthralling, epic narrative spanning six decades and spotlighting some of the most vivid events and characters of our times. 'Enormous imagination and vitality . . . a huge book in every way' – Bernard Levin in the *Sunday Times*

The Penitent   Isaac Bashevis Singer

From the Nobel Prize-winning author comes a powerful story of a man who has material wealth but feels spiritually impoverished. 'Singer . . . restates with dignity the spiritual aspirations and the cultural complexities of a lifetime, and it must be said that in doing so he gives the Evil One no quarter and precious little advantage' – Anita Brookner in the *Sunday Times*

Paradise Postponed   John Mortimer

'Hats off to John Mortimer. He's done it again' – *Spectator*. A rumbustious, hilarious new novel from the creator of Rumpole, *Paradise Postponed* is now a major Thames Television series.

Animal Farm   George Orwell

The classic political fable of the twentieth century.

A CHOICE OF PENGUIN FICTION

Maia   Richard Adams

The heroic romance of love and war in an ancient empire from one of our greatest storytellers. 'Enormous and powerful' – *Financial Times*

The Warning Bell   Lynne Reid Banks

A wonderfully involving, truthful novel about the choices a woman must make in her life – and the price she must pay for ignoring the counsel of her own heart. 'Lynne Reid Banks knows how to get to her reader: this novel grips like Super Glue' – *Observer*

Doctor Slaughter   Paul Theroux

Provocative and menacing – a brilliant dissection of lust, ambition and betrayal in 'civilized' London. 'Witty, chilly, exuberant, graphic' – *The Times Literary Supplement*

July's People   Nadine Gordimer

Set in South Africa, this novel gives us an unforgettable look at the terrifying, tacit understanding and misunderstandings between blacks and whites. 'This is the best novel that Miss Gordimer has ever written' – Alan Paton in the *Saturday Review*

Wise Virgin   A. N. Wilson

Giles Fox's work on the Pottle manuscript, a little-known thirteenth-century tract on virginity, leads him to some innovative research on the subject that takes even his breath away. 'A most elegant and chilling comedy' – *Observer* Books of the Year

Last Resorts   Clare Boylan

Harriet loved Joe Fischer for his ordinariness – for his ordinary suits and hats, his ordinary money and his ordinary mind, even for his ordinary wife. 'An unmitigated delight' – *Time Out*

A CHOICE OF PENGUIN FICTION

Stanley and the Women   Kingsley Amis

Just when Stanley Duke thinks it safe to sink into middle age, his son goes insane – and Stanley finds himself beset on all sides by women, each of whom seems to have an intimate acquaintance with madness. 'Very good, very powerful . . . beautifully written' – Anthony Burgess in the *Observer*

The Girls of Slender Means   Muriel Spark

A world and a war are winding up with a bang, and in what is left of London all the nice people are poor – and about to discover how different the new world will be. 'Britain's finest post-war novelist' – *The Times*

Him with His Foot in His Mouth   Saul Bellow

A collection of first-class short stories. 'If there is a better living writer of fiction, I'd very much like to know who he or she is' – *The Times*

Mother's Helper   Maureen Freely

A superbly biting and breathtakingly fluent attack on certain libertarian views, blending laughter, delight, rage and amazement, this is a novel you won't forget. 'A winner' – *The Times Literary Supplement*

Decline and Fall   Evelyn Waugh

A comic yet curiously touching account of an innocent plunged into the sham, brittle world of high society. Evelyn Waugh's first novel brought him immediate public acclaim and is still a classic of its kind.

Stars and Bars   William Boyd

Well-dressed, quite handsome, unfailingly polite and charming, who would guess that Henderson Dores, the innocent Englishman abroad in wicked America, has a guilty secret? 'Without doubt his best book so far . . . made me laugh out loud' – *The Times*